THE MID-MORNING MURDERS

To Martha

BARA S. ROSENHECK

Bara S Rosenheck

DEDICATION

This book is dedicated to my wonderful husband, Arnold Rosenheck, who has been my support and helper. Through thick and thin, he's been there as my cheer-leader and best friend.

ACKNOWLEDGEMENT

Many people have given their time, insights, and suggestions to me while I was writing The Mid-Morning Murders. I especially want to thank Julie Harris for her great support and encouragement. Julie provided invaluable assistance.

CHAPTER 1
SUSAN JEFFREYS

Returning home from her morning Pilates class, Susan Jeffreys was lost in thought. As she approached her pedestrian-only street, commonly found in many Venice neighborhoods, she swung her car to the rear alley that gave access to her garage. She sat in her car for a few minutes, reviewing her lengthy "to-do list."

First, she'd need to clear the kitchen of the breakfast mess left after the family's hasty departure to school and work, and her own rushed exit to get to Pilates class on time. Next would be the laundry, planning dinner, picking up the girls from school, and a trip to the dentist with ten-year-old Cindy. Oh- and she had also promised to pick up Stan's clothing at the dry cleaners. She could do that after Cindy's dentist appointment since she would pass right by the cleaners on the way home.

Susan's usually clean and tidy kitchen was unfortunately just as she had left it, a chaotic mix of dirty breakfast dishes, crumbs on the table, and a half-full carafe of coffee. "Oh, good," she thought, the coffee's still warm and I'm going to enjoy a second cup." Relaxing with the rich brew she glanced at the clock, calculating the time she needed to get her work done. She checked the week's calendar of activities and the social commitment that she and Stan had scheduled: Saturday night dinner at the Wilson's house, Monday night a parent-teacher conference at the girls' school, and next Thursday a meeting with their accountant to deliver receipts, and forms, needed for their tax return preparation.

She smiled. Her life was filled with joy and these simple mundane tasks were blessings. Life was good, and she was thankful for what others might consider a quiet, perhaps boring lifestyle. Her home in Venice, in a newly gentrified area, was located near the pedestrian promenade that attracted so many tourists year-round. Susan delighted in living in a beachfront community that offered so many wonderful activities. She never needed fame, wealth, or excitement to be happy. Instead, she took pride in her role as wife, mother, friend, and a good neighbor.

The highs of a successful career, the excesses of wealth or fame, all meant little to her. Susan knew she had a good husband and adoring children, a stable and secure existence.

Although Susan had carefully planned the day's chores, none of them would be completed despite her well-ordered logistics. In fact, the only planning done this day would be carried out by her surviving family members--planning for her funeral. Clearing away the final specks of crumbs on the table Susan placed her coffee cup in the dishwasher and proceeded to the bedroom to pick up the laundry basket she had prepared earlier then headed for the laundry room. After her housekeeping tasks were complete, she intended to go to the market and pick up some groceries needed for dinner.

Carefully sorting the laundry, she thought she heard a sound. Was it the wind through the open window rustling the curtains? Perhaps it was the icemaker dropping some cubes into the collection bin in the freezer? More likely it was the next-door neighbor's dog digging in the dirt separating their two yards. Susan reassured herself that it wasn't anything to worry about and continued her sorting. The house was quiet; her mood was positive. Humming to herself as she moved through the house, she never suspected these thoughts would be her last.

Jason moved swiftly. Susan only glimpsed his shadow as the bullet struck her chest. She was dead before she hit the floor.

Satisfied he had achieved his goal, Jason leisurely tidied up. He collected the pieces of laundry scattered by her fall. He carefully replaced the towels, undergarments, and workout clothing in the basket and set it on top of the washing machine. Next, he retrieved the 9mm bullet casing, placing it in his pocket. He meticulously cleaned the spilled detergent that had splashed on the countertop as she fell, making sure he left no trace of the liquid soap. There was no need to worry about fingerprints; his gloves, put on before he entered the house, assured there would be no link to his identity. Jason was in no rush. His plan was perfect, and he knew the house would be empty and undisturbed for several hours. It was mid-morning. He hadn't had time for breakfast, so he decided to see what was in the well-stocked refrigerator. He was pleased to find his favorite brand of yogurt, some fresh crusty bread, a half-empty carton of milk, and some cheese.

Seating himself at the kitchen table he leisurely enjoyed breakfast and once finished, made sure to pocket the spoon he used. The now empty milk and yogurt containers, he carefully placed in his backpack.

Jason took some time to look around the house. Nice. Solid middle class, he thought. There were some photos of Susan's family on the mantel. He studied a picture of Susan, surrounded by her husband and children, that must have been taken at some ski resort where he assumed the family had recently vacationed. There were other pictures of the girls, taken at various ages, showing them maturing from toddlers to pre-teens. The man in the photos, Jason assumed, was Susan's husband, and he appeared nerdy but solidly middle class.

After a brief tour of the premises, Jason checked around once more to make sure all was clean and neat. No fingerprints, no utensils, no food containers that might indicate DNA was left behind. Content that all was as he had planned, Jason quietly let himself out the side door of the garage, the one through which he had entered. He strolled down the suburban street softly whistling a tune. It was a very productive start to a lovely day.

CHAPTER 2
WILL PRESTON

Will Preston rode his bicycle home from the church meeting. He loved this bike ride, not only because it was good exercise, but also because it gave him the chance to enjoy his beautiful community. He savored the smell of the clean fresh air and the aroma emanating from the flowers and trees as he slowly passed the green, well-maintained lawns and gardens in his neighborhood.

The church meeting had been short, allowing him to return home well before the lunch hour. Now that he was retired, he enjoyed his civic involvement and the ability to participate in church activities and other community events. As an active member in the nearby Pasadena branch of the NAACP, he was well respected by both his African American and white friends and colleagues.

Between his involvement in church activities, his activism with the NAACP, and frequent workouts at one of the local gyms, his days were full. His build and appearance reflected his commitment to health and fitness. He was a large man, muscular and powerfully built. During his years of employment, his workouts had to fit into his busy schedule, but now, in retirement, he could get a workout in more frequently and on a regular basis. He appeared much younger than his sixty-seven years. He was convinced that his years of eating right, exercising, and enjoying a satisfying career contributed to his health and positive mental attitude.

Will decided to take the scenic route home and entered the park that separated his house and his church. As he peddled through the park, he thought about the new woman in his life and smiled. It had been five years since he became a widower and although the loss of his beloved wife still pained him, he had come to the realization that it was time to move on. He and Shirley met at an NAACP event last year and there was an instant connection. They had much in common and a friendship soon developed. More recently, a deeper bond was felt by both. Their romance and sexual closeness amazed him. He had been unaware that people in their sixties could still kindle a flame of desire and he delighted in this newly learned truth.

The park was lovely, quiet, and empty at this hour of the morning. Jason, dressed in camouflage, was well concealed by the foliage, and moved silently through the park's greenery. Children who frequently populated the park were in school and it was too early in the day for the picnickers.

Traffic in the park was light and Will Preston slowed his bike to an easy pace relishing the solitude. The first bullet hit him in the back of his head, the second tore through his lower back. His body and bicycle fell to the side of the road resting on the grass near a flower bed. His blood formed a sticky pool on the dark blacktop of the park roadway and stained the patch of grass on which his body rested.

Jason retrieved the spent Smith and Wesson 9mm casings and placed them in his pocket. He checked the laces on his jogging shoes, making sure they were secure. It was a beautiful day and the perfect environment for a jog. Earlier, Jason had scouted out the many jogging paths in the park and had decided which one he would follow. He chose the three-mile circle; the one closest to his car in the parking lot near the park entrance. Returning to the car before his run, he stashed the gun away in the glove box. Looking around and seeing no one in sight, he took a few minutes to stretch and warm up.

He had never visited this park before and thought it a wonderfully inviting place for the residents of Santa Clarita to enjoy. It not only had jogging trails and picnic areas, but also some tennis courts and a baseball diamond. He made a mental note to try and return at some time in the near future and enjoy the park's amenities and bucolic environment. Maybe he'd bring a date and they'd barbeque and picnic before a run.

He started his run slowly, not exerting or taxing himself. He entered a shady area lined with tall trees and the smell of rich earth. Jason's life was on track. He felt good. The Jeffreys kill, back in January, and the one this morning went as planned. He left no clues. As he quickened his pace, he thought about his next move. Perhaps he'd send a mysterious anonymous letter to the police or the newspapers, taunting them for their stupidity.

Jason thought about his heroes as he ran. There was The Zodiac Killer who had taunted the police with his letters. Then there were the letters from Gary Ridgeway, known as the Green River Killer, and those sent by Dennis Rader, the BTK Killer; BTK for blindfold, torture, and kill. That last one made him laugh.

Now he broke into a sweat as he entered a hilly area. No, he decided, it was too early to send any communication. The stupid authorities didn't have any idea what was going on and he wasn't about to tip them off. He didn't need to send letters or engage in any torture crap to prove his point or to make headlines. Jason would just quietly and efficiently continue doing what he was doing and enjoy the satisfaction it brought him. Jason continued his run, his mind wandering to his tormented past.

He recalled his active, fit youth, his promising career as an athlete; his goal to become famous. Jason felt he had been unfairly victimized by his overbearing parents. He cursed them for their demands of perfection. They had relentlessly pushed him to succeed and were harsh disciplinarians, resulting in his becoming withdrawn, sullen, and angry. Now that fate had made all his plans an impossibility, his fury and disappointment were calmed by engaging in violent acts. His ego and his narcissism enabled him to justify what he had done and would soon do again.

CHAPTER 3
Julia Horner: Past and Present

Julia glanced at the kitchen clock and was happy to see she still had enough time to grab a cup of coffee and read some of the day's news before she'd head off to her office. The headline in the paper grabbed her attention: "Another Murder in Southern California."

The newspaper's account seemed to imply that the unsolved murders recently reported were connected and might be the work of a serial killer. Authorities claimed that this was just speculation and at the present time there were no leads to indicate the murders were linked in any way. They stressed that there was no reason to believe the victims had anything in common and there appeared to be nothing linking any of the crimes.

Julia found this of interest but dismissed the theory of a serial killer. During her career practicing law, she had defended accused murderers. Some she believed to be innocent, and others she believed guilty. But she knew serial killers usually followed a pattern. They sought victims of similar appearance, or they killed using similar methods, or they had a motive that was common to each victim. As reported in these articles, nothing suggested any common ground. Julia also recognized chances were good that the paper had exaggerated a connection between the crimes that didn't exist.

Although Julia had defended men accused of murder, she believed serial killers were a whole different breed than the killers she had interacted with in the past. Serial killers' motivation stemmed from some sickness she couldn't understand and was unrelated to the greed, jealousy, or hatred of unfair employers or unfaithful lovers, usually expressed by her defendants. As a court-appointed pro-bono attorney she accepted these cases but knew she could not defend a serial killer if asked to do so. She shuddered at the thought of ever meeting such an individual.

Reading these news accounts triggered fearful memories of her own victimization at the hands of a brutal rapist. Shaking her head, she unsuccessfully tried to erase the ten-year-old memory. Ten years? Julia shook her head, wondering how time could have flown by so quickly. So much had transpired since then that Julia needed to sit down and organize her thoughts and quiet the memories racing through her head. Those years had included periods of great joy, as well as dark days, hovering between fear and despair.

Much of Julia's anger and frustration stemmed from the police department's unwillingness or inability to arrest a suspect. Sam Malloy, the detective in charge of the case repeatedly told Julia there was no evidence and no proof to substantiate her claim that she had found, and could identify, her attacker. After questioning the man Julia accused, but finding nothing suspicious, Julia and Detective Malloy frequently clashed over her insistence that Danny Patterson be arrested.

Fate, she thought, has a way of seeping into every aspect of one's life, complicating the future. The twists and turns of events paved an unlikely path that led Julia, the victim of

Patterson's brutal beating and rape, to become his legal guardian and custodial caregiver!

Many months after assaulting Julia, Patterson ironically became a crime victim too. An attack by two aggressive muggers left him a quadriplegic with brain injuries that kept him in a minimally conscious state most of the time. Only occasionally was he aware and alert. Needing institutional care, he became totally dependent on others.

Never arrested, never charged with the crime, and never punished by the legal system, Patterson's future was placed in Julia's hands. If these circumstances were portrayed in a movie, Julia knew the audience would appreciate the irony of her assailant languishing in her care. This was an improbable situation, but the only avenue through which Julia finally realized justice.

During several periods of clarity, Patterson came to understand his dependence on his caregivers, not only the nursing home employees but also his total dependence on his conservator, Julia Horner. He was unable to fend for himself due to his paralysis, and he periodically vacillated between awareness and a comatose state that lasted for long periods of time.

When conscious, he knew it was Julia Horner who made his medical decisions, managed his finances, and represented his interests. Appointed by the court, she held his power of attorney, and therefore controlled his medical treatment and financial future. Julia often wondered if her assailant understood the complicated circumstances that allowed the court to appoint her as his custodial caregiver.

Now, after ten years of functioning as Patterson's guardian, Julia was notified that her ward had passed away in his sleep. The letter notifying her of his passing was placed in her desk file with other documents concerning Patterson's care. On the surface, the documents appeared to be a clear example of a patient/caregiver relationship and gave no hint of the sinister and complicated connection between the two. Heaving a sigh of relief and recognizing this was the final chapter in their chaotic association, Julia turned her attention back to the newspaper that triggered these memories.

Yes, she thought, Patterson was one of the bad guys, but nothing, thank God, like a serial killer. "I pray I never cross paths with one of them! I've had my fill of criminal minds and intend to steer clear of lawbreakers from now on," she muttered aloud. Julia had no way of knowing that would be far from the truth. Her silent prayer to remain uninvolved in criminal investigations notwithstanding, she soon would find herself in the midst of great danger.

CHAPTER 4
DETECTIVE ROBERTA PHELPS

A month had gone by since the Venice Pacific Community Police Station notified the Los Angeles Police Department of the murder of Susan Jeffreys. A small beach, and residential community, Venice rarely encounters a murder crime, and as protocol demanded, a case of this magnitude is referred to the Los Angeles Police Department's Robbery-Homicide Division (LAPD/RHD). Detective Roberta Phelps was assigned to the case.

Experienced and meticulous with detail, Detective Phelps enjoyed a good rapport with her colleagues and was well-liked and respected for her excellent work. In her early fifties, Detective Roberta Phelps enjoyed the energy of a twenty-something. Silver streaks of hair, mixed with her black locks, gave her a distinguished yet youthful appearance. She was black, soft-spoken, and determined to successfully resolve whatever case was thrown her way.

After viewing the crime scene and studying the photos; interrogating the deceased's husband,

Stan Jeffreys; talking with neighbors, and meeting with the medical examiner; Detective Phelps was stymied. There seemed to be no leads and no clues. Whoever this perp was, he or she was just as meticulous with detail as she.

She felt great sympathy for the bereaved husband. And after questioning him and doing the necessary verification, Phelps concluded he had an airtight alibi. The poor guy was at work and in full view of his coworkers at the time of the murder. Phelps was also able to conclude that the family had no financial problems, there didn't appear to be "another woman" in Stan Jeffreys' life, and there wasn't a hefty insurance policy on his wife.

Continuing her due diligence, the detective learned there was no discord in their relationship, no affairs, or any other irregularities that might be motives for murder. Of course, Detective Phelps would keep digging and was open to changing her conclusions when and if other information was uncovered. But at the present time, the Jeffreys family seemed to be a quiet happy family; enjoying the fruits of their labors; living an ordinary suburban life.

After a very long day reviewing the Jeffreys case files and listening again to the recorded conversations Detective Phelps checked her notes and shook her head. Always an optimist, she believed eventually this case would be solved and the murderer brought to justice, but, she mused, this one might take a while and cause some additional gray hairs. As with all her cases, Phelps was determined to follow up on all possible leads and decided she would drive down to Venice again in the morning just to make sure nothing was missed. She placed the case files in her briefcase, deciding to review them one more time after she got home.

Roberta was bone tired. After trying to dig up helpful information, she reluctantly admitted she had turned up nothing new. Now in midlife, she was just as sharp and committed to her job as when she graduated from the Police Academy. Yet periodically thoughts of retirement crept into her head. She and her husband, Mark, envisioned a quieter life, perhaps in a retirement community. Or better yet, on a houseboat docked at some peaceful tropical island. They did this daydreaming half-heartedly, knowing full well they would probably die of boredom and never could separate themselves from the careers they loved; careers that gave them so much satisfaction. Retirement was only a far-off fantasy, and if good health and youthful stamina prevailed, neither were ready to make any changes.

Roberta and Mark first met at the police academy and quickly bonded. Careful not to draw attention to their romance, they managed to function as a couple and only close friends were aware of their relationship. Now, working in separate precincts and with unrelated job responsibilities, their marriage was no longer considered unusual or controversial.

Frequently they discussed various aspects of their work and bounced ideas and theories back and forth. They loved the opportunity to share ideas and enjoyed the stimulation of inquiry and debate. It also helped each of them to clarify points and explore differing views of troubling cases.

Lingering at the dining room table they discussed the day's activities. "What's going on in your head?" Mark asked. "Looks like you're very engrossed in something troubling," he continued.

"Yeah, it's that Susan Jeffreys case in Venice you heard about. I know it's early, but nothing seems right about it. No clues, no motive, no leads. I'm sure something will turn up, but as always, I want things to happen yesterday."

Mark smiled reassuringly calling her by his favorite nickname. "Listen, Funny Face, if there's anything to find, you're the one who will find it. Just give it time and your usual careful attention. You know what you're doing, and things will fall into place. You know the routine, slow and steady."

"You are the best!" Roberta replied quietly, looking up at her husband, Mark, thankfully. Smiling, she lovingly mouthed the words, "I love you."

After a satisfying dinner and a good night's sleep, Roberta felt refreshed and anxious to continue sorting out what might have happened to cause this heinous crime. This time, her discussion of the case with Mark had added little to her sketchy understanding. She would just have to heed his advice and take one step at a time.

As Roberta drove to the crime scene in Venice the next day, she mentally outlined her work. She decided she would investigate the victim's activities on the day of her murder. According to the husband's account, Susan Jeffreys left for her Pilates class at about the same time he and the children left for work and school. Reports from the morgue indicated Susan Jeffreys was killed shortly after returning home. Roberta was going to question the Pilates instructor and others in the class to see if they could add any new information.

The instructor told Detective Phelps that Susan regularly attended her class, loved the workout, and had many friends in the group. Not much to go on. Phelps learned the victim was a good athlete, was physically fit, and had no enemies.

After canvassing the neighbors and questioning the merchants Jeffreys frequented, Detectives Phelps was still disheartened. She updated her notes to include the information acquired during the day's few interviews, but Phelps realized she currently was facing a dead end.

Returning to her LA office, Phelps studied the ballistics report on the Jeffreys murder. The fatal bullet was a 9mm bullet, fired from a handgun. Thousands of gun owners use this common bullet and this information, although important, would provide no help in finding the killer.

CHAPTER 5
JASON MONTGOMERY

Jason sat on the bed, legs crossed, with his iPad resting on his thighs. He was completely engrossed in his video game, almost unable to direct his attention to anything else. He viewed the screen as if it was the center of his life, the focus of his existence. Totally absorbed in the animated action, he periodically called out instructions or demands.

"Get him, you cocksucker. That's it! Cut him down." Jason shouted. His thumbs moved rapidly over the keys and his body shook as he listed first right and then left trying to direct the hero's movements.

"Good job, another score," he hooted.

Exhausted, Jason wound down his game just as his cell phone rang. It was Bill Sneed, the fitness center manager. "Wuz-up, Bill?" Jason asked.

"We have a new gym member, a guy named Rob Winters, who's looking for a personal trainer," the fitness manager told Jason. "Claims he's just moved into the neighborhood and is looking for a new gym and trainer. Says he's always worked out and had a gym membership, but because of his move, he needs to change his membership. Looks about right; fit and active and seems to have a few bucks. Since you're the trainer who's up at bat next, here's his number, and if you're interested give him a call."

"He's probably another loser," Jason sighed. "But I'll call him later and see if he can pay the tab." No need to rush he thought.

Disconnecting the call Jason scowled. Another fat-cat who thinks he's a great athlete. Jason rapidly invented a fantastic persona, creating an entire scenario about the unknown Rob Winters. "Bet he thinks he's God's gift to women, this muscle-bound ape. Bet he's just another superhero who needs to keep in shape so he can rule the universe," he said out loud. His unbridled mania convinced Jason that this prospective new client could not be trusted. "He's probably a spoiled pretty boy who takes his looks and ability for granted." Continuing his one-sided conversation with the empty room, his rage escalated.

His unrealistic speculations were based on Jason's many previous clients. Over the years, he had to deal with some who were deadbeats and never paid for his time or help; others were bullies who refused to follow his instructions and insisted on using heavy gym equipment incorrectly and dangerously. Jason reasoned he had to constantly protect himself from these idiots. The thought of some of his past female clients, who were too timid to try anything, "afraid of breaking a fucking fingernail," made him sneer in disgust. Jason only concentrated on the clients he considered worthless, overlooking the many who paid on time and worked well with him.

He checked the calendar on his phone. He liked to schedule private clients for the morning hours so he could go to the gym in the afternoons or evenings. Most of these jokers liked to work out early anyway so they could get to their jobs on time, and that suited Jason's schedule just fine. The working stiffs were easy to schedule early and the retired bums and housewife bimbos he could schedule in a bit later, say before noon. He decided to call Rob Winters later.

Grabbing a protein drink from the fridge, Jason dropped down on his worn sofa. He lazily reviewed his recent scores, the ones he considered his job to eliminate. He thought about his victories, ridding the world of the deadbeats and time-wasters who were dumb enough to believe personal trainers could transform them into god-like creatures. Oddly, Jason's most recent victim, Will Preston, didn't fit this mold.

Preston was in decent shape, and he had a good exercise routine. He wasn't a slacker, but he just rubbed Jason the wrong way and Jason decided he needed to get rid of him.

Some of Jason's clients were fitness center members, but others had no gym affiliation and had been referred to him by word of mouth. Jason killed four or five of his slower-moving patrons years after their acquaintanceship ended. Susan Jeffreys fell into that category. His recent visit with her, in her laundry room, occurred years after they stopped working out together. But when he learned the dumb broad was taking a Pilates class, he knew Pilates couldn't replace a real workout. It pissed him off, so he decided to get rid of her.

Taking a large gulp of his drink, Jason issued a low gruff laugh thinking about poor old Al Sanchez, another one of his former clients who Jason eliminated. Sanchez would never transform into an Olympian, especially after having a heart attack. Did Sanchez really believe working out with a trainer would keep him in shape and improve his ticker? A dumb doctor probably convinced Sanchez exercise would improve his health. Jason realized shortly after they began working together that Sanchez had no potential and would be a drag on society. Jason waited several months and sure enough, just as he expected, Sanchez canceled their future workouts claiming that, although his stamina seemed to improve, he was disappointed that he hadn't lost any weight. It was then Jason knew he had to end Sanchez's disappointment by taking his life.

Jason knew about disappointment. It stays with you, never leaving your side or memory. He bitterly remembered his disappointments. A natural athlete, gifted in many sports, Jason was a superstar at school. At a very young age, his potential as a future Olympian was recognized, and he was recruited and groomed by the best coaches and trainers. His parents sacrificed for his training, and he worked night and day to perfect his skills, strength, and techniques.

Promised he would one day be a successful athlete, with his photo on a Wheaties box, at a tender age he was convinced medals and trophies would someday line his shelves and he would have endorsements and contracts up the wazoo. Now Jason believed those who trained and advised him were liars.

His disappointment eventually turned to rage when an injury left him without a future! Suffering several broken bones and torn tendons after a serious fall, Jason underwent three surgeries to repair the damage. As his body continued to mend his need for retribution grew. Months of physical therapy followed, but it was undeniable that his athletic career was over. During his period of recovery, he became withdrawn, angry, and vengeful. He convinced himself that life was unfair, and he wanted payback.

His unsympathetic parents blamed him for the mishap. Repeatedly they criticized him for not being cautious, for not paying attention to his movements, for not succeeding. Their scathing indictments of his inability to overcome his injury left Jason filled with contempt for any criticism. He vowed he would find a way to get even.

Jason's grief over his lost potential produced violent behaviors. He killed and mutilated small animals. He started a fire in a neighboring yard. His cruelty and brutality increased as he grew more fixated on the unfairness of his loss. Without remorse, he experienced pleasure from his reprehensible behaviors.

And so, after his recovery, Jason worked as a personal trainer. He liked working as a trainer but quickly learned many of his clients didn't pass his assessment of their worthiness of his time and attention.

Many of his clients were deserving of a good trainer. They were the ones who worked hard and put effort into their exercise program. The others expected miraculous results far beyond reasonable expectations and were lazy or uncommitted. Jason deemed them unworthy of his training or tolerance. He thought them losers; they reminded him of his painful background and what could have been. It was his responsibility, he thought, to get rid of them.

Somehow, reviewing these deeds calmed and relaxed Jason but his tranquility was interrupted by the shrill ring of the telephone. "Shit. Who the hell is that?" he wondered. He decided he'd get rid of this intruder as soon as possible.

"Yeah? Who is this?"

"Hello. This is Rob Winters. I'm calling because…

"How did you get my number?" Jason sharply interrupted. "I'm supposed to call you."

"Yes, I know, but I thought I'd give you a call first. I got your number from one of your former clients, a friend of mine, Will Preston." Jason's voice went flat, and his face turned white.

"Will Preston, you know Will Preston?"

"Right. I'd like to set up a meeting to discuss my fitness goals and your experience and approach. Then we can decide if working together would be a good fit and we could look at our schedules and your fees."

Jason's mind was spinning out of control. This was an ominous unexpected crisis. He silently cursed and felt a cold rush of fear. He didn't want to be connected to Will Preston in any way. Jason hated loose ends and he knew this loose end had to be tied together and eliminated quickly. Jason's options flashed before him. He could hang up; he could deny Will Preston was a former client of his... or he could kill Rob Winters.

CHAPTER 6
STICKING POINTS

The two men sat at a small corner table, in the crowded Coffee Bean and Tea Leaf Café. Jason Montgomery was more than a little nervous but Rob Winters, seated across the table from Jason, seemed relaxed as he nonchalantly draped his tall body over his chair. With his legs outstretched and his arms carelessly thrust across the table, he could not have guessed what was going through Jason's mind.

Paying no attention to Rob's description of his workout routine or athletic history, Jason instead, was concentrating on what his next moves should be. Life or death for Rob Winters?

"I like to put in about 45 minutes on the treadmill, that's if I can't get to run outdoors," Rob droned on. "I'd like to build some muscle on..."

"Shut the fuck up. I don't give a shit," Jason thought but said nothing. His eyes glazed over, and his face revealed a distant, detached look. Jason shook his head as if in agreement with

Rob's detailed description, but Rob's litany of goals and fitness needs made absolutely no impact on Jason. All of Jason's concentration centered on if and when he'd have to kill Rob.

Killing Rob or letting him live was a dicey choice. Either one needed to be carefully considered. If Jason eliminated Rob, and the friendship between Rob and Will Preston were ever discovered, their connection could lead investigators to Jason. After all, the investigators would soon realize that both men used the same trainer. That was one argument against taking Rob out.

On the other hand, allowing Rob to live could lead to other problems. Once Rob learned of Will Preston's murder, he'd surely ask Jason questions or worse yet, suggest the police question him.

As Rob continued talking about his goals, his desire for physical improvement, and his athletic achievements, Jason pondered his damage control options. Rob Winters was a problem, an obstacle. Alive or dead Winters was a liability and Jason realized he had to craft a solution.

Breaking his silence Jason cut into Rob's recital. "How do you know Will Preston and when did he give you my number?" he asked.

Rob was aware that Jason hadn't heard a word of what he was saying, and he also recognized Jason's far away glassy-eyed detachment. Jason wasn't the only one making decisions. Rob was also evaluating Jason and he wasn't sure he wanted to have anything to do with him. Jason appeared disinterested and evasive. Unlike other trainers Winters had hired in the past, Rob had the feeling Jason was a phony or was hiding something. He was unable to identify exactly what disturbed him about Jason's demeanor, but he had the distinct feeling he couldn't be trusted.

Jason's behavior was strange, and Rob was quick to understand that Jason wasn't the trainer he wanted to hire. In the back of his mind, Rob wondered why Will Preston had recommended Jason. He decided he'd call Will and let him know he wasn't impressed. Believing this meeting was a mistake and a waste of time, Rob drained his coffee cup and tried to end the meeting.

"Well, thanks for meeting with me Jason. Let me look over my schedule and your fee scale and I'll call you when I'm ready to make a commitment," Rob said.

Jason wasn't ready to be brushed off without gaining the information he wanted. "So, tell me," he repeated his question. "How do you know Will Preston and when did he give you my number?"

"Oh, we worked together years ago, before he retired. We haven't kept in touch regularly, but we do speak now and then. I'll give him a call and let him know we met," Rob said. "I know Will would like to hear that we met. After all, he's the one who suggested I call you."

CHAPTER 7
Family Time

Julia's eight-year-old twins, Bobby, and Hillary sat at the kitchen table finishing their last bites of breakfast. "Don't forget to take your lunch boxes. They're here on the counter for you," she reminded the children.

"What did you pack, Mom?" Bobby asked. "

"Oh, just all the things you love: mussels and snails and puppy dog tails," she joked.

"No, no Mom. I'll be really hungry, and I want a good lunch," Bobby protested.

Hillary laughed and placed her hands over her mouth, now full of the cheerios she was finishing. Julia winked at the kids giving them a thumbs up.

"Have I ever packed you a bad lunch?" she asked.

The kids returned the thumbs up and were all smiles. Julia also smiled, knowing the twins were bright, happy, well-adjusted kids, popular with peers, and doing well in school. Julia and her husband, Matt, were lucky as hell to have produced these marvelous offspring while their own adult lives spun in circles. Now that Danny Patterson would be out of their lives for good, Julia felt relieved that her responsibility as his conservator was over.

Years earlier, before they married, Julia and Matt's lives were upended when Julia was viciously attacked. It was during her long period of recovery that Julia vowed to find her rapist and bring him to justice. Finally, several months after the attack, a serendipitous meeting at Julia's law firm brought the two together in the same room for a meeting with her boss. Learning he was due to inherit a large sum of money from his foster mother's will, Patterson appeared unannounced in Julia's law office. It was then she was able to identify Patterson from a scar on his hand, as her tormentor, her rapist. The police found her identification unconvincing and had no evidence linking the accused to the crime. The detective on the case, Sam Malloy, explained there was little likelihood a trial could end with a conviction.

Ironically, freed from police scrutiny, Danny Patterson moved on to continue his criminal activities in Las Vegas. Julia was devastated when Patterson wasn't arrested. Detective Malloy repeatedly maintained that there was no chance of a conviction.

Paradoxically, Danny Patterson became the victim of an aggressive mugger and sustained a serious life-threatening injury. Finding Julia's business card in Patterson's pocket, the Las Vegas Police contacted her and she, the only person they could connect to the comatose victim, was eventually appointed by the court to oversee his care. Requiring a conservator and without any relatives, the court, in a bizarre twist of fate, chose Julia to become his conservator simply because she had acted as his attorney in the past when his foster mother's will went through probate.

Fully aware of Julia's reluctant connection to her rapist, Matt couldn't wait for news of her ward's demise. Matt hated the man with a passion and resented Patterson's hold on Julia. Matt remembered the dark days when Julia was tormented and threatened by him, and then finally became obligated to care for him. With the news of Patterson's passing, they hoped life would become less stressful.

Julia's work was fulfilling and financially rewarding. Over the intervening years, she looked for more challenges and attended courses, studying criminal psychology, and studying forensics. Always concerned that equality and justice were well served, Julia vowed to do all within her power to assure those goals were achieved.

As a partner in the law firm of Winthrop and Gallagher, Julia enjoyed a busy and challenging professional life. She loved her work and was regarded as an outstanding lawyer. Her reputation was envied by many who held her in high esteem and valued her friendship, even when they were on opposing sides of a case and there were several courtroom clashes where she was pitted against a colleague who argued convincingly trying to unravel the case Julia had just presented. Frequently, after showdowns like these, the two sparring attorneys met for a glass of wine to recement their kinship!

Putting the past to rest was the goal Julia and Matt hoped to achieve as soon as possible. The sad history of Julia's rape and subsequent responsibilities as a caregiver could now become a distant memory and their life together could become so much less complicated.

With a sigh of relief, Julia readied herself to leave for the office. Although troubling, the recent news headlines about the unsolved murders in Southern California were not her concern and had nothing to do with her history or her resolve to lead a quiet life.

Neither Julia nor Matt could possibly imagine how their future would become inextricably tied to the serial murderer responsible for the unsolved deaths reported in the news. Feeling optimistic about the future, Julia left for her office.

CHAPTER 8
CLOSURE

It was a perfect Sunday morning; the kind of lazy morning one dreams about. Julia and Matt sat at their kitchen table and marveled at the beauty of the day and the splendor of their manicured garden. The kitchen table, placed near the window, provided the pleasure of viewing the bursting rose bushes, the busy hummingbirds, and the tranquil water fountain with its cascading waterfalls. The gently falling water softly fell into a large basin that rippled as birds splashed and then flew away. It was hypnotic.

Matt and Julia's young twins, Hillary, and Bobby were in an upstairs bedroom playing Monopoly, while Julia and Matt savored their quiet time together. Relaxed, after a hearty breakfast, Matt took Julia's hand and affectionately stroked it.

"How are you doing sweetheart?" he asked. "I know you struggled with the responsibility of the Patterson's guardianship, but now that he's passed away, that burden is gone. I hope you can let it go, and file those bad memories away with that letter from the nursing home. Let all the reminders of him be laid to rest. You've fulfilled your obligation to oversee his care, and now you're free."

Julia smiled, appreciative of Matt's concern and support. This sensitivity was characteristic of his dedication to her wellbeing. Over the years Matt was her rock, her protector. It was more than a decade ago when Patterson randomly grabbed Julia in the park and left her for dead. He had no idea who his victim was and didn't care.

Recovering from the trauma of the rape and beating was only one part of Julia's battle to regain her mental health and independence. Perhaps the more difficult obstacle was her attempt to prove Patterson's guilt to Detective Sam Malloy.

Although the police had no evidence and no clues that might point to any culprit, Julia knew her attacker's voice and speech pattern, and visible tattoos. If the police found him, she could identify him. But the police never found the suspect. Instead, Julia found him!

Over the ensuing years, Julia never forgot that her attacker walked into her law office claiming to be the missing heir to a three-million-dollar bequest. Danny Patterson's deceased foster mother left him the money. At the time, his whereabouts were unknown, and Julia's firm was trying unsuccessfully to locate him. One of the many complications in locating the missing heir was his use of aliases to disguise his criminal past. Hiding under assumed names, Patterson was able to stay one step away from detection.

Reading the obituaries, Patterson learned of his foster mother's death, and it was then he decided to visit Julia's law office, claiming his inheritance. Julia immediately recognized him as her attacker. He had no idea it was she who had been his victim

It was irrefutable that he was indeed the beneficiary. Proving his guilt to Detective Sam Malloy was far more difficult. Julia met with Malloy many times and insisted she knew her attacker's identity, but Malloy stood firm. There were no clues, no evidence, and no reason to issue a probable cause warrant.

After months of disappointment and depression, Julia realized her accusations would lead nowhere. Ultimately, Patterson left her office with a three-million-dollar inheritance, her business card in his pocket, and a smile on his face.

Before his departure, Patterson repeatedly threatened Julia demanding she withdraw her accusations and tell the police she was mistaken about his involvement. Waving her business card in Julia's face he menacingly warned her of retribution if she continued to pursue his arrest. His threats and stalking frightened her, but she remained committed to seeing justice prevail.

Matt was proud of his wife's bravery and stamina in confronting both Patterson and Detective Malloy. He applauded Julia's ability to accept the fact that Patterson would be a free man and a wealthy one to boot. But Matt had difficulty understanding Julia's willingness to accept the responsibility of becoming Danny

Patterson's conservator when he was unable to function on his own.

Shortly after Patterson's clearance of any wrongdoing, his destiny was sealed. Barely surviving a violent mugging, Patterson suffered paralyzing injuries and neurological complications.

"Matt, I love you and I treasure your devotion and never ending support. It's been a long hard road for both of us. I agree, it's been a tough experience and I know you have questioned some of my decisions, but I promise you there will be better days ahead for us, now that Patterson had passed on." She sighed and added, "The entire ordeal was more than ten years ago, and you're right, it's time to let it go."

Julia's eyes clouded over as she started to clear the breakfast table. Talking about the dreadful history of those years nearly brought her to tears, but she believed Patterson's passing would bring closure.

"Okay now. Let's get the kids and plan something fun to do today. It's beautiful out and maybe we can have a picnic in the park."

She quickly finished the breakfast dishes and packed a delicious lunch for the family. As they readied to exit the house, their departure was interrupted by the ringing phone.

Julia was shocked to hear the voice on the other end of the line. She never expected to hear from this person straight from her past. The caller was a man she hated and never wanted to speak to again. Her hands shook as he spoke, and she listened with a feeling of dread.

Much to her chagrin, he insisted he wanted to meet with her to discuss their prior relationship. He was a powerful figure who, in the past, exerted pressure on her producing frustration and fear. It had been ten years since they last spoke and since that time Julia hoped her future life would be free of his interference. She vowed not to be drawn into this man's negative influence again.

Of course, Julia had immediately recognized the caller's voice. "Hello Julia, this is Detective Sam Malloy. It's been a while, but I want to talk to you." Determined to maintain her now safe, secure life, Julia hesitated before responding to his insistence that they meet.

CHAPTER 9
MEA CULPA

Detective Sam Malloy was suffering pangs of guilt. Several years had passed since his retirement, but memories of the Julia Horner case haunted him. Looking back at his notes and records, Malloy knew he had done his best to find the rapist who had attacked and beaten her, but there just was nothing to go on. Try as Malloy might, he couldn't uncover any evidence linking the man Julia Horner accused to the crime. Still, the years-old unsolved case bothered the detective.

Strolling around his cozy cottage, Malloy sipped his coffee and talked, as he often did, to his Golden Retriever, Maisie. "Well, Maisie, I did all I could, but my hands were tied. She claimed she was certain about his guilt and after she identified him, we questioned him."

Malloy lowered himself into a kitchen chair and quietly reviewed his recollections of the case. "Yup, we did all we could, but Ms. Horner believed there was a miscarriage of justice." Pausing to refill his coffee cup, Malloy continued.

"Unfortunately, after questioning him we realized we had a "he said, she said" scenario and nothing else. She thought she found the culprit, but we had no proof. If you don't have enough evidence for a conviction, you're stuck."

Maisie answered by wagging her tail and lazily curled up on the floor next to Malloy's chair.

"It's bothered me for years and I believe I owe Ms. Horner an explanation and apology. She was scared to death by her assailant who threatened and intimidated her, but there was little we could do to protect her." Malloy took in a deep breath and another sip from his coffee cup.

"You see, Maize," he continued, "we had nothing but her chance encounter with him months after she was attacked. She claimed he waltzed into her law office and, BAM! She recognized him as the phantom who attacked her in the park. How do you prove that?"

Maize rested her head on Malloy's shoe. It was then that Sam Malloy decided to call Julia Horner and offer a mea culpa for his inability to solve the crime that had changed the course of her life. Since his retirement, Malloy was bothered by the outcome, the lack of closure. Although he was unsure of the response he might receive, Malloy was sure calling her and offering some explanation was the right thing to do.

Malloy got up from his chair and continued his stroll around the room. "All I can tell you is she was convinced he was the perp. I don't know or care what happened to him. After we questioned him, we had to let him go. But her anger and dismay have left a bad taste in my mouth."

Malloy knew Julia was now a partner in the law firm of Winthrop and Gallagher, where she started her career as an inexperienced legal apprentice. Malloy hoped that, with the passage of time, and with more experience, Julia had come to understand he could not have arrested the person she identified. Surely, she would understand that with so little to go on, the prosecutors felt no urgency to pursue an indictment in a case with little chance to win a conviction.

Swallowing his last sip of coffee, Malloy also hoped that over the years Julia had developed a thicker skin, a forgiving nature, and a willingness to see that his hands were tied. "Who knows Maisie? Perhaps she's stronger now and that entire bad experience produced a firm backbone."

With Maisie as his audience, he rehearsed his presentation. "I called to say I'm sorry," he told the dog. "No, no, that's not right. I didn't do anything to be sorry about." Malloy took another minute and started again, "I called to give you an explanation. No, that's not right either." Too clinical and unfeeling, he thought.

"You've been on my mind, and I thought I'd say hello." Ridiculous, he decided. "Maisie, this is harder than I thought, why can't I get this right?" he said.

With feelings of doubt and some hesitation, he lifted the phone. He decided to be direct and would simply say there were things that needed to be discussed. He would ask Julia Horner to join him for a drink and some forgiveness.

CHAPTER 10
DETECTIVE STEVEN RICH

Detective Steven Rich loved his work. He had been with the LAPD for several years and was considered one of the outstanding detectives on the force. He had an impressive number of arrests and convictions and took great pride in his ability to solve tough cases. The latest one on his desk was the murder of William Preston.

Detective Rich spent several weeks reviewing the information collected in the Will Preston case. It seemed the victim had no enemies and was well-liked. Rich theorized this murder might be a random act of violence, or perhaps a hate crime perpetrated by a White Supremacist. Will Preston was known to be an activist in the local NAACP, and it was conceivable he was targeted because of his race and activism. The detective decided to further investigate some of the far-right hate groups that operated in his jurisdiction.

The Golden State Skinheads, The American Freedom Party, and The Daily Stormer were groups Rich would take a closer look at. All three had chapters in Southern California and were known to espouse violence against minorities. The detective thought any one of their members might be capable of committing this murder. He made a note to talk with the appropriate officers in charge of monitoring these hate groups.

Unfortunately, there was not much information Rich could share with them other than the fact that the victim was a Black man. The only thing that might provide a lead was the fatal bullet was a 9mm slug, fired from a handgun. Nothing else had been found at the park crime scene that could assist in finding the gunman.

After meeting with his colleagues in the Hate Crimes Division Rich, and they as well concluded the involvement of members of these groups was unlikely. The scuttlebutt they heard didn't indicate they were planning any violence. Certainly, Rich knew the police would continue to monitor these groups, but at the present time, their participation in this crime seemed doubtful.

Steven Rich was not one to give up easily. This case bothered him. What could be the motive to kill someone like this victim? Well-liked, respected, unassuming Will Preston must have pissed someone off. Greed, jealousy, hate, money, power, theft, were the usual motives the detective was most familiar with, but Preston's death wouldn't provide anyone with either benefits or satisfaction. What was the motivation? Who stood to gain from his murder?

In the middle of the night, Rich wandered around his empty house weighing all feasible scenarios. He spent his few off-duty hours at home mulling over his notes concerning the life and death of Will Preston. Worn out due to a sleepless night, the detective reviewed all he knew about the crime. At three in the morning, he sat down with a bowl of cereal and milk and continued to think about the clues, or rather the lack of clues.

It was five years ago that he and his wife had divorced, and now that he lived alone, he believed some of his best insights were developed while others were fast asleep. He liked the quiet and solitude the midnight hours granted. Freed from the hustle and bustle of the police station and its distractions, Rich's understanding of each case evolved and his grasp of each set of circumstances improved. Nevertheless, he reasoned that at this late hour the precinct would be quiet.

Already wide-awake Rich decided to shower and shave and return to his cubby at the police station. Peering at his image in the mirror, he paused and took a minute to evaluate his appearance. "Not bad," he said to himself with a laugh. He was a good-looking man and looked younger than his forty-three years. His thick black hair showed no gray, his build was muscular, and his crooked smile gave him the appearance of someone who was confident and self-assured but still capable of self-deprecation.

The detective's thoughts returned to the case. Nothing made sense, including the possibility of a random drive-by shooting, because there was no evidence of car traffic in the area of the crime. The murder happened on a bike trail in a heavily wooded area that could not accommodate vehicular traffic. Perhaps the shooter was also riding a bike?

Making a mental note to confer with his colleagues, Detective Rich left for his office. He would get together with Detective Roberta Phelps who was working another tough case with few clues. Both cops were frustrated by the lack of evidence in their assigned cases and perhaps if they bounced some ideas around, they could gain some insight. Rich was aware Roberta was struggling to find clues in the Susan Jeffreys case that occurred some months earlier, and he hoped they could work together to puzzle out the pieces on both the Jeffreys and Preston cases.

Periodically, the LA detectives met jointly to swap ideas, brainstorm, and discuss the cases each was working on. Meeting with Roberta was not unusual, and they mutually respected and liked one another. It was Rich's hope that Roberta might shed light on this most troubling case. She was a no-nonsense cop, as committed as he was to leave no stone unturned.

Despite his hopes that discussing the Preston case with others in the department would be helpful, he still had a nagging worry that there was more underlying this case than met the eye. Murders in the community of Santa Clarita were rare. This wasn't a crime of opportunity; it was too well planned. There was no home invasion gone wrong, no sexual assault, no.....nothing. This just looked like an isolated case of the victim being in the wrong place at the wrong time when some lunatic randomly fired a gun. What other explanation could there be?

Rich continued to run the "what if" scenarios through his head as he drove downtown. He sincerely hoped this one wouldn't end up in the unsolved dead-end cold case file. It angered him just knowing that try as they might, there were some cases the police couldn't solve because no clues and no leads were ever revealed. He viewed his work not just as a professional commitment, but also as a personal quest to uncover the truth. As a young rookie, he vowed he owed it to each victim to seek justice for them and closure for their families. He wouldn't renegue on that promise. His strong allegiance to justice and the law compelled him to strive to meet those goals.

Swinging his car into a parking spot, he grabbed his notes and entered the precinct, greeting his coworkers. He spotted Roberta Phelps talking to the captain and waved a warm hello.

"Hey, Roberta," he yelled across the room, "Any chance we can have coffee together? I'd like to run some thoughts by you. I have a tough nut to crack that's driving me up a wall. I'd like some input from you."

That afternoon Rich and Phelps grabbed a coffee break and some quiet time. Interestingly, both their cases seemed to have similarities but few links to establish a connection. Both victims were well-liked, not involved in any love triangles, had no debt or drug connections, and had no large insurance policies.

All would have been normal motives for these crimes. Who might benefit from their deaths? Neither victim had disgruntled employees nor jealous ex-spouses.

Coincidently, both Jeffreys and Preston were killed by a 9mm bullet but neither detective believed there was anything else that might connect the two victims. It was apparent Susan Jeffreys, the white middle-class housewife and mother, had no link or association with Will Preston, the retired older Black activist. Experience led both detectives to conclude these two crimes were isolated unrelated murders.

CHAPTER 11
DICK STEIN

Jason arrived early at the CVS located just off Sunset Boulevard in West Hollywood and parked his car. He knew Dick Stein, his least favorite client, would be late again. No matter how many times Jason warned Dick about his tardiness, "Dick, the Prick" never learned. "Dick, the Prick" had become Jason's unspoken mantra each time he silently referred to Dick Stein. Stein's tardiness was just one of Jason's grievances and the list of reasons he disliked Stein was long. Jason was sure Dick was gay, and if that wasn't reason enough for Jason to dislike him, it was compounded by the fact that his payments for Jason's services were often late.

It was unusual for Jason to agree to meet a client and carpool together to a hiking location but when Dick requested, really begged, Jason, to drive, he reluctantly agreed. In hindsight, Jason realized this was a good idea. He had decided to eliminate Dick and the two of them going off together to some distant location made sense to him. Not having to worry about Dick's vehicle being at the scene might slow discovery of his body as well as an investigation.

The trip to Vasquez Rocks was only about forty minutes from West Hollywood and Dick insisted that was where he wanted to hike. The natural park was perfect for Jason's needs and provided secluded areas, well hidden from view. The rock formations extended over more than 900 acres offering hikers and rock climbers several levels of difficulty. Most visitors roamed and climbed the formations closest to the parking lot but there were formations and trails more distant from those most often visited. Stein was strong and fit, but because he was such a pain in the ass, Jason decided that his days should be numbered. When Stein told Jason he wanted to hike at Vasquez Rocks, Jason researched the area and decided it was the right location to eliminate him. Jason calculated that if they hiked to some outlying edge of the park, he could get rid of "Dick the Prick" there, and it would be weeks, perhaps months before the body was discovered.

The two men had been working out together for several months and Jason quickly became weary of Stein's constant prattle and demands. Last month, claiming boredom exercising in the gym, he wanted to try rock climbing and insisted Jason find an indoor facility offering that option. Before that, he demanded Jason swim laps with him in a pool located in a distant YMCA. Stein's exercise whims and constant demands enraged Jason and he concluded he wouldn't put up with any more of his dictates.

The Vasquez Rocks setting was a wonder. The largest of the rock formations was used as backdrop scenery hundreds of times in scores of western movies. Jason smiled as he remembered viewing countless movie cowboys charging across this landscape pursuing the bad guys. This time, Jason would direct the drama.

Arriving at their destination Stein asked, "Okay pal, are you ready to hit the trail? I hope you're ready to meet the challenge, otherwise, I'll leave you in the dust."

"Quit the BS, Dick, you're not that good." Jason's dislike of his client intensified when these exchanges pitted each against the other. Pointing in the distance, Jason indicated a destination and the direction in which they would head. Dick squinted at what looked like the horizon but accepted what obviously would become a competition. "Okay, old man, let's do it."

The trail was rugged, and Jason had chosen this path knowing few others would undertake such a difficult route. Within minutes both men were sweating. The morning sun was bright, and the heat of the day was already beginning to climb. They pushed on, increasing the distance between themselves and the few tourists who came and left once they had taken a few photos of the landscape.

The two hikers marched on only stopping occasionally to quench their thirst as they guzzled water from bottles that dangled from their belts. The trail was steep and littered with loose rocks. Plumes of dust rose as brief gusts of wind encircled them, almost hiding them from view. Now breathless, they pushed on, neither wanting to show the other signs of fatigue.

Reaching the pinnacle of a rock formation, Jason and Dick eased themselves to the ground and rested, each leaning on a boulder. They were now so far from the parking area and visiting tourists, Jason felt confident his murderous plan would be undetectable. "Dick, there's a shady ledge just on the other side of this pile of rock. Let's go down a few feet and grab some R&R down on the other side," Jason suggested.

Jason's Smith and Wesson 9mm M&P M2.0 handgun, now outfitted with a silencer, was concealed beneath his vest. Nevertheless, Jason reasoned the sound of the gunshot would be further muffled by the rock wall separating them from the main area of the park. Slowly and carefully both men inched their way down the steep formation displacing loose rocks and debris. This far side of the rock pile was rugged, and it was more difficult to move down than was the trek uphill. Extreme caution was needed to maintain balance. The rocky slope had no cleared footpath to follow and they descended slowly. Exhausted, both men sat on the small shady ledge. As Dick reached for his water bottle, Jason drew his gun.

At the sight of the gun, and totally surprised by Jason's unexpected movement, Dick instantly responded rising to his feet, and with one forceful maneuver lunged at Jason, catching him off balance. A full head taller Dick towered over his attacker. Both strong athletes, each was determined to overpower the other.

Lunging at his assailant, Dick, like an enraged bison, headbutted Jason causing him to stumble, fall and drop his weapon. Scrambling away from Dick, Jason lost his footing nearing him closer to the edge of the overhang. Gaining traction Jason retrieved the gun and struggled to an upright posture.

Simultaneously, Dick grabbed a large rock and violently struck Jason above his right eye. Blood cascaded from the blow blurring Jason's vision, clouding his mind but he clung to the weapon.

The battle continued. Dick, a former college wrestler, threw Jason to the ground and tried to pin him. Placing his knee on the wrist of Jason's hand, the one holding the gun. Dick pummeled him again with the large rock. Jason, stunned by the blow, tightened his grip on the gun, and with a surge of strength, wriggled free and escaped Dick's hold. Grunting and sweating both men continued to fight.

With muscles straining and adrenaline pumping, they exchanged blows and curses. The fight for survival continued; first favoring one, then the other. Both men were aware they were fighting for their life, and neither would yield. These well-matched warriors endured battering blows, hammering each other relentlessly. Now, both standing upright, each grabbed the other in their Herculean efforts to overpower their opponent.

The sound of the gunshot was barely audible. Dick crumpled to the ground, bleeding from the chest.

CHAPTER 12
OLD NEMESIS, NEW COLLEAGUE

The restaurant was hidden away in a small but upscale shopping center. It was nestled between a hair salon and a liquor store and was a snug little resting spot. The storefront windows revealed a cheerful interior, boasting chintz tablecloths and small vases of colorful flowers decorating each table. It was one of Julia's favorite places and whenever she lunched there, she felt as if she were entering an oasis of peace and tranquility. She asked for a table where she could watch the customers as they entered the restaurant, wanting to give herself time to settle herself before Malloy entered.

It was a place familiar to her and she knew it would help her try to relax in Detective Malloy's presence. All her previous meetings with him had filled her with consternation and the feeling that he didn't believe a word she said. She wondered why on earth he would want to see her now, after all these years?

At first, Julia was reluctant to accept his request to meet. She said all she had wanted to say to him in the past, and she was sure he knew she wanted nothing more to do with him. He represented a history she wanted to forget, a chapter she thought was closed. But curiosity had gotten the better of her, and although somewhat hesitant, she agreed to meet with him.

Julia decided she would say little and just listen. She would not express any warmth or friendship and would only display a cold exterior, replacing the frightened young women he had known her to be in the past. Julia was older now, more mature, more experienced than the victim she had been. Malloy's interviews in the past filled her with frustration and she believed there was no justice in his soul.

When Detective Malloy entered the restaurant, Julia experienced a rush of surprise. He appeared older, a bit grayer, and far less intimidating. Julia saw a smile of recognition cross his face as he approached her table, and he extended his hand in greeting. His demeanor was anything but threatening and it seemed he wanted to acknowledge an old friend.

Julia responded with a very formal, "Hello Detective Malloy," and said nothing else.

"I'm retired now, please call me Sam. I'm just a plain old civilian who wants to make amends," he said, hoisting himself into the chair across from her.

"What exactly does that mean?" Julia coolly asked.

Before Malloy could answer their server appeared and asked what they wanted to order. Julia and Malloy both were grateful for this interruption as it gave them time to collect their thoughts.

They each studied the menu, made their choices, and dispatched their server back to the kitchen only to return a few minutes later.

After a brief but awkward silence, Malloy took his leap of faith. "Julia, I owe you an explanation; not really an apology because I was a by-the-book cop. It's been more than a decade since we last spoke, and your rape case is still open. I believed everything you claimed, and I tried my hardest to back you up, but the evidence we needed to make a solid case just didn't exist."

He paused enabling her to digest his words. "Even though you were sure you knew who your attacker was, we couldn't prove it and the possibility of a conviction was very doubtful." Lowering his eyes and his voice, Malloy's bearing confirmed his honest regret that he couldn't arrest the man who had violated and then threatened Julia. They both sat in silence for a few minutes digesting the importance of this statement.

Continuing with his explanation Malloy let Julia know he had no idea what had happened to the man she accused. "Julia, I just want you to know I'm sorry we couldn't give you closure."

Listening to Sam's mea culpa, Julia's frame of mind softened. It was obvious the past troubled this retired cop as much as it troubled her. Julia felt comfortable allowing this discussion of the past to end here with a mutually agreed upon decision to make amends and let the past go.

For a fleeting moment Julia thought she might tell Sam she knew her attacker's fate, however, she wasn't ready to share that part of her story. Not just yet. Perhaps at some time in the future, she would allow Sam Malloy to learn that for more than ten years Julia controlled and directed the life of her attacker, Danny Patterson.

Julia smiled a smile of knowing acceptance as lunch arrived. "So, let's move on to more timely crimes," Julia suggested. "Have you been following the news reports about these unsolved murders in Southern California?" She asked.

"What else does a cop do in retirement?" He quipped. "It's fascinating but really puzzling. The different cases may be related but there's little to tie them together."

"I've been following the news accounts also," Julia volunteered. "I have more than a passing interest in forensics and criminal psychology. Over the years I was involved in some research and also took a boatload of psychology courses studying serial killers and other criminals with personality disorders." Julia paused, waiting for Sam's reply.

"Really?" Malloy's interest heightened. "And do you have any theories because the cops surely don't," he asked leaning in closer. "I'm sure they'd like to hear from you if you can assist. Perhaps you could call the Tip Line? I know the police would love to hear from you," he joked.

Julia frowned. "That's not funny Detective Malloy. "If you can't take me seriously, there's no need to poke fun."

Malloy hastily apologized, realizing he had taken the wrong approach. He desperately wanted Julia to understand he respected her intelligence and sincerely wanted to hear any theories or possibilities she could offer.

"Well from what I've read serial killers usually have a pattern and a preferred victim profile. Ted Bundy killed women and girls. Jeffrey Dahmer victimized boys and men. David Berkowitz, known as Son of Sam, went after women with long dark hair while they sat in parked cars in lover's lanes.

"Woah, is that coming from meek little Julia Horner?" Malloy asked in amazement.

"I've been studying," Julia said. "Serial killers usually follow a chosen path. Some kill only prostitutes or the homeless. Others prefer to prey upon gay men."

"Where are you going with this?" Sam questioned. "Do you see a connection? As far as the cops know, there doesn't seem to be one. One victim was a white middle-class housewife, another an older Black man, a third was a middle-aged Hispanic. There were other victims but there seems little linking them together."

"I have some ideas. Nothing concrete, but I've been giving it some thought," Julia said.

Malloy measured Julia's words and thoughts before saying more. Taking a breath, he volunteered some information.

"Julia, even when I couldn't act upon your past accusation, I respected your intelligence and gut feelings. And now you've piqued my curiosity once again."

Sam paused and then continued. "Julia, I'm meeting a former colleague, Detective Roberta Phelps, LAPD, tomorrow at 4:00 for drinks. She's working one of these unsolved murders. How about joining us?"

CHAPTER 13
ONE SMART COOKIE

It was obvious Roberta Phelps and retired Detective Sam Malloy had a deep respect and affection for one another. They warmly embraced and greeted each other like two old friends and colleagues. Julia watched this reunion and patiently waited for Sam to introduce her.

"Julia, come here. I want you to meet one of the best cops in LA. She's an impressive tough gal who the force is lucky to have. We worked in the same precinct for years."

Sam's introduction of Julia was no less impressive. "Roberta, this is Julia Horner, a friend and outstanding attorney I've known for years. Unfortunately, she and I lost touch and hadn't seen each other for quite a while but we recently caught up and I think she's someone you'd like to know." Sam continued, praising Julia's law accomplishment and knowledge of criminal behavior until Julia started to blush and quieted him down.

"That's enough," Julia said emphatically. "Stop, I'll just send her my resumé," she joked.

"Any friend of Sam's is a friend of mine," Roberta countered. "And if he is so impressed with your accomplishments, I'm convinced they are enviable and extraordinary. I've worked with Sam long enough to know he tells it like it is."

The three of them sat at a small table in the dimly lit bar. Their drinks arrived as they continued exchanging stories of cases they worked together and the histories of their careers. Julia contributed to the conversation recounting some of her more interesting courtroom victories and even included some of her disastrous errors made early in her tenure at the law firm.

Sam, Roberta, and Julia laughed at these shared memories and voiced feelings that ranged between pride, regret, and nostalgia. Sharing these emotions drew them together and began to cement a comradery that would last, binding them into a small but cohesive group of friendly colleagues.

Finally, Sam revealed the reason he invited Julia to join them. "So, Roberta, what's the scuttlebutt on these murders that are filling the headlines? It looks like there have been a few that were committed with a 9mm gun. Do you see anything else connecting the crimes?"

"To tell the truth, there have been more than the three most recent murders. We have a few cold cases that involved a 9mm handgun but have no clues. We think the same gun was used in each of the killings but there's been nothing else to tie them together," Roberta reported.

Sam let out a small whistle. "That's not been reported in the news. So, you believe it may be the work of one hitman. The public's been kept in the dark about that fact. The same gun. Hmm."

Turning toward Roberta, Sam swiveled in his chair closer to her. "Roberta, I asked Julia to join us because she has a background in forensics and the psychology of serial killers. She has some theories that might be helpful."

Roberta looked doubtfully at her friend. "Sam, you know we can't discuss what's going on with a civilian. The only thing we can talk about is what's already been reported."

Sam let out a belly laugh. "Roberta, it's me you're talking to, and you just said it may be the work of one perp. And Christ, police even talk to psychics if they think it will be helpful."

"Yes, but you know…"

Sam interrupted, "Julia has credentials as an officer of the court and as a legal professional. She can be trusted. I think you should hear her out."

Acquiescing, Roberta shook her head in agreement. "All right, what's your take on all this?"

Taking one more sip of her drink Julia cleared her throat and took a deep breath. "I've only followed the three most recent murders that were reported in the news. They are the Susan Jeffreys, Al Sanchez, and Will Preston cases. I don't know anything about other murders, but

Roberta, you mentioned there are several cold cases where the same 9mm gun was used?"

"Yes," Roberta acknowledged.

Julia continued, "From what the papers report, those three victims were engaged in some kind of physical activity. They were athletes or workout enthusiasts or were attempting to achieve some level of fitness."

This grabbed her attention and Roberta leaned forward, closer into the conversation. She quietly asked Julia to continue.

"I don't know why this connection jumped out at me but reading each news account I realized that Jeffreys' Pilate's instructor was questioned, Preston's body was found near his bike, which he reportedly rode regularly, and Sanchez's wife said he had started a fitness regimen after having some heart problems. It just clicked in my mind, and I thought it an interesting connection," Julia said.

"The percentage of Americans who exercise regularly is low. I think only about 20% of the population meets the suggested physical activity recommendations made by the Center for Disease Control. Because so few adults work out regularly, I thought it intriguing that all the victims were involved in some kind of fitness activity. That may be more than a   coincidence."

At this point, Detective Roberta Phelps took out her notepad and started writing. It was clear she was interested in what Julia had to say and Roberta would seriously consider the possibility of this connection. Roberta took notes as Julia continued.

"Roberta, I'd investigate the habits of the cold case victims and see if any of them exercised or worked out on a regular basis. This may be a link." Roberta drummed her fingers lightly on the tabletop but was quiet for a few minutes. Closing her notepad Roberta looked at Julia, before responding.

"Well, there's a lot of food for thought here. It's an interesting theory and one I'll follow up on. One of my colleagues, Detective Steven Rich, and I have been looking for links to connect the victims and this is one we hadn't considered." Finishing her drink, Roberta continued, "This is a new twist we'll definitely explore." Turning toward Sam, she added, "Sam, your friend Julia's one smart cookie."

CHAPTER 14
HOMEWORK

Julia was ecstatic that her recent meeting with Detective Phelps went so well. Phelps assured Julia that she and Detective Rich would consult with her on an ongoing basis. This possibility gave Julia a feeling of power and purpose. If she could contribute to solving these murders, her long-felt frustration about past legal injustices might begin to dissipate. The memory of her own rape and attack still lingered and she knew the wheels of justice stopped turning due to the lack of evidence. Proof turned those wheels— accusations only clogged them.

If proof was the answer to injustice Julia vowed, long ago, to diligently do what she could to support the rights of those who had been harmed by finding evidence of the crimes committed against them. She had a deep faith in the law, and as a lawyer, she understood the rules and boundaries imposed on those in positions of authority. Believing she had a moral obligation to pursue justice and accountability, she felt compelled to aid the police.

With each passing day, Julia studied the news reports checking to see if any new murders fitting a similar profile had been committed. She eliminated from her growing files reports of husbands who killed wives, murders committed by burglars, and murders committed for wealth or some kind of revenge. She carefully recorded anything she thought might be relevant to what had now been dubbed by the press as, "The Mid-Morning Murders."

"How is Miss Marple doing today?" Matt asked as he entered the room. For days now, Matt had been calling his wife by the name of one of fiction's notable detectives. Julia wasn't sure if he was making fun of her or merely trying to relieve her tension. Yesterday, he repeatedly referred to her as Sherlock. Julia was beginning to feel if she didn't love him so much, she just might want to murder him!

"Okay, smarty pants. I'm doing my homework for my upcoming meeting with Detectives Phelps, Rich, and Malloy."

"No kidding? Have there been any new leads?" Matt asked.

"Well, there's one new step forward. Roberta Phelps and Steven Rich both work in the same LAPD station and they've been comparing notes on the individual cases they've been working," Julia explained.

"And what have they come up with?"

"Phelps is working the Jeffreys case and Rich is investigating the Will Preston murder," she explained. "Neither of them could find anything in common except the 9mm slugs used until they realized all these murders were committed during the mid-morning hours."

This grabbed Matt's attention and he became more interested. "Did they follow through on your recommendation to look into the fitness activities of each victim?" he asked.

"Absolutely, they did. They also looked into the backgrounds of some cold case victims, and it looks like there's a real connection here. All of them either had gym memberships or participated in some kind of exercise class or fitness program. The locations of the various facilities differ, but there's a strong possibility this is the link the police have been searching for."

"Agatha Christie, I'm so proud of you!"

"Matt, stop that or you'll be next on the "Mid-Morning Murder" list, she joked. "I wish you'd take this more seriously. I'm really trying to assist the police with these difficult cases and right now I have no sense of humor. Please stop teasing me. I know you mean no harm but stop it!"

"I am serious." He protested. "I know you're doing something important, but I just want you to stay safe and not become so involved that it upsets or endangers you in any way." Matt came closer and kissed his wife's forehead and gave her a warm hug.

"There's no way I could possibly be in danger Matt. Why do you think I'm at risk?" she asked. Matt didn't answer but he had a nagging premonition that his wife could indeed be drawn into a dangerous web.

CHAPTER 15
PSYCHOPATHS

Julia was both intrigued and delighted at the prospect of working with the police. The invitation to join the team gave her a sense of purpose and she was confident her hunch regarding a connection between the several unsolved murders was correct. She hoped to convince the authorities these crimes were the work of one individual. She was sure there was a connection and assumed the killer worked alone. The more she thought about the murders, the more connections she saw. All the deaths occurred during the mid-morning hours and in her mind, Julia, like the press, had already dubbed the events The Mid-Morning Murders.

If the police agreed it was the work of one perpetrator, a Task Force might be formed, and perhaps the FBI would be called in. Julia would not be an official member of a Task Force but would work with them as a consultant, providing insight and tips. Because of the still uncertain connection between the crimes, the police officials were reluctant to use the term serial killer and therefore decided it was not yet necessary to call in the FBI. Nevertheless, they worried an investigation might lead them to that eventuality and they were grateful for any additional help Julia and Sam might provide.

Julia's knowledge, coupled with Sam's years of experience, could provide the understaffed and overworked police with the additional resources they might need to resolve this case. The police brass, those higher up in the administration, had approved Julia's and Sam's informal, unofficial participation. As agreed, they would receive no remuneration, would take their instructions from Task Force officials, should one be formed, and back off when told to do so.

Although Julia shared her knowledge and educational experience about serial killers with Phelps and Rich, she knew she had to review her notes and brush up on her facts. Quite a few years had elapsed since her graduate school studies and Julia realized she needed to hit the books once more.

She had been a good student. She had shared her expertise with the detectives but wanted to make sure her information and understanding of serial killers was current. In addition to devoting time and attention to her academic textbooks, Julia frequently checked the FBI web pages to review the latest theories and findings regarding the psychological makeup and characteristics of this specific group of criminals.

The police had not officially acknowledged these deaths were the work of a serial killer and Julia had to make sure her instinct was right, and her conclusions were on target. She had one week to master all the information before the next meeting with her colleagues, and she spent most of it reading and note-taking.

Fortunately, she was able to clear much of her workload at her law office so she could throw herself tirelessly into preparation for the next meeting with Phelps and Rich. Aware the police were not convinced a Task Force was needed, Julia knew if she were to present such a scenario, she had to be prepared that they might. Searching her bookcase and older school files, she dug out and quickly reviewed her notes and research from years past. Feeling somewhat hesitant about this new role, and needing some reassurance, Julia reached for the phone.

"Hi, Sam. I've been thinking about our seats at the police table," she joked. "I'm brushing up on my knowledge and hope I'm equal to the task. We can't make any mistakes and must be sure of all our facts."

"Of course, you're equal to the task," Sam assured her. "You already proved your metal by providing the right direction to their investigation. They'll be happy for any additional leads we can provide."

"Gee, I hope you're right. I've been looking over the FBI's web pages and reports, and read that when a Task Force is formed, investigative consultants may be used. It also states that a list of all resources and experts needed should be drafted and maintained. I guess we'd fit into that category."

"Yeah, they'll need all the help they can get. In my experience, it's the best and most experienced homicide detectives that are assigned the roles of Task Force lead investigator and co-investigator. That would be Phelps and Rich, and with our relationship with them, I know they would value our contributions."

"Well, it's one step at a time," Julia thoughtfully added. A Task Force may be formed. It's up to the law enforcement agency handling the case to make that call. The FBI and input from their Rapid Response Team agents may not be called upon."

"Right," Sam agreed. "We could work with the police on an informal basis and if we make progress and find the needed evidence, there would be no need to ask the FBI for assistance. And that, my friend, is our task."

Satisfied with Sam's reassurance, Julia returned to her notes. She divided them into two categories. The first focused on the psychological and emotional characteristics of serial killers; information she had found on the FBI website. The second focused on the structure of an investigation, the role of administration, and the role of the Task Force agents.

The FBI website contained a lot of information about serial killers, but what resonated with Julia, when considering this case, was that serial killers generally kill at least three people, about one month apart, in different locations, and that the killer might be targeting a certain group. Anger and revenge are frequent motives. Inherently they are narcissistic, selfish, and arrogant. Believing that they possess superior intelligence, their low level of tolerance for people they determine to be "worthless," leads them to feel murder is justified, and further, that they will not be apprehended.

Julia also consulted "Comprehensive Psychiatry" Vol. #56, January 2015 and reviewed the information about serial killer's that was described in that study

Julia put her books and notes aside. She sat quietly at her desk and thought about the future. Believing she was compelled to continue down this frightening path made Julia's head hurt. Deciding that she needed a break, she left her desk and headed into the kitchen, for a cup of tea. Sipping the hot liquid, she began to relax.

She was beginning a new role. Thinking about how she was becoming the mythical crime fighter she fantasized about in her youth was both amusing and terrifying. Briefly, she recalled her mother's advice, "Be careful what you wish for..."

"Yes, Mom," she thought. "I always wanted to solve crimes, pursue the criminal, and find justice. Now that I have a chance to do all that, it is scary.

The investigative opportunities that lay ahead of her filled her with an equal portion of excitement and dread. She shared her insights and learned from those with investigative experience. She'd be on the borderline between safety and danger because, of one thing she was certain – she would not, could not, only remain at a desk discussing theories. If she was going to engage in this undertaking, she'd go full throttle and do what she felt necessary. Finishing her tea, Julia returned to her notes and began reviewing the FBI recommendations. With a small sigh, she wondered if she'd have been better off with a stiff drink instead of the hot tea. Sleepy but determined to continue she returned to her desk.

It was at this point that Julia's eyes began to glaze over. But she was forced to focus on the serious nature of the position she was about to fill. None of this information was new to her but reviewing it drove home the overwhelming responsibility she was accepting.

She readied herself for bed. Brushing her teeth, she studied her reflection in the mirror above the sink. Was she ready for this challenge? Was she prepared for any danger that might result from her involvement? Could she help find the Mid-Morning Murderer?

CHAPTER 16
CONNECTING THE DOTS

Detectives Phelps and Rich parked the car and sat for a minute reviewing their phone conversation with Rob Winters. Finding his voice mail message on the deceased Will Preston's phone, they had contacted Winters. Both detectives were experienced enough to know this meeting with him might not provide any new information about the Will Preston murder, but they were determined to leave no stone unturned.

Phelps and Rich worked well together. For the past several weeks, the media had been reporting that the Mid-Morning Murders had the police stymied and frustrated, which resulted in increased anxiety and concern about the bad press. They considered it a giant step in the right direction when the top police brass acknowledged that the recent murders and several cold cases might be connected to one another, and therefore had approved Phelps and Rich teaming up to work jointly on the cases.

The idea that the murders could be connected was fostered by Roberta's friends Sam Malloy, and Julia Horner. When Roberta shared it with her superiors, she credited her colleagues. Consequently, at several meetings, Malloy and Horner were in attendance with Phelps and Rich as they presented a compelling argument that the victims were all engaged in workout and exercise programs. They theorized that this common thread was the long-sought connection. The only missing puzzle piece was the point of contact that linked them all to the killer.

The detectives slowly made their way to Rob Winter's apartment hoping he might provide additional information. He sounded cooperative when they spoke on the phone setting up today's interview. Rob Winter's apartment spoke volumes. It was a small neat little place and as soon as they entered, it was immediately apparent a well-heeled upwardly mobile junior executive lived within. Pricey knick-knacks were strategically placed on bookshelves that also contained leather-bound volumes of the classics. The artwork was minimal but expensive. The color-coordinated navy and grey upholstery, floor coverings, and painted walls reflected a refined masculine taste.

Roberta started the conversation. "Mr. Winters, as you know we are investigating the murder of your friend, Will Preston. While inspecting his home we listened to the message you left on his home phone."

"Yes," Rob replied. "I called him. Of course, I didn't know of his death at the time I made the call. I hadn't spoken to him for a while, and I left a message hoping he'd get back to me. It was quite a shock when I learned he was murdered."

"We're sorry for your loss. Where you two close?" Roberta inquired.

"No, not close but we did know each other. We worked at the same place and occasionally ran into each other at the gym."

"What made you call him out of the blue?" Detective Rich asked.

"Well, it really wasn't out of the blue. I asked the manager of my new gym for a referral, and he gave me the name of a personal trainer." Rob took another minute to organize his thoughts before continuing.

"Then I remembered that, some time ago, Will gave me the name and number of a trainer he used in the past and it was the same guy. I wanted to let Will know that I met with him. I also wanted to give Will feedback about the meeting and to ask his opinion of this guy, because I wasn't impressed with him."

"Why?" asked Detective Rich.

Rob thought for a while before answering. "I don't know, he seemed kind of strange. He didn't express any interest in me or my fitness goals. I've had other trainers in the past who were really into hearing about my workouts and exercise levels, but he appeared to be concentrating on something else. It was like he wasn't interested in booking a new client. He was just weird."

"Can you give us his name and contact information? We'd like to talk to him. Perhaps he can give us more insight into Will Preston's habits and routine." Roberta got out her notepad, ready to take down the information.

Rob shuffled through his iPhone address book. Finally, finding the requested information, he paused before responding. "I do think this guy is an oddball, but I don't want to get him into any trouble. And I certainly don't want him to know I was the one who gave you his name."

"Mr. Winters, we can assure you, you will not be mentioned at or connected to any interviews with the trainer." Steven Rich gave Rob a reassuring smile. " Our sources are confidential. We'll tell him that we found his contact info in Mr. Preston's phonebook and we're interviewing all the people listed."

"Well, okay then, but please leave my name out of it. The trainer's name is Jason Montgomery and here's his number." He showed Roberta the number on his iPhone. Returning to their car, the detectives discussed their notes and confirmed they accurately reflected the conversation. Winters seemed honest and straight-forward but was not eliminated from a list of possible suspects.

Indeed, that list had grown after the police combed through Will Preston's papers, phone contacts, and address books.

"Steven, did you catch the fact that this Jason Montgomery was not listed in any of Preston's address books?" Roberta asked her partner.

"Sure did. Perhaps Preston was wise enough to want to distance himself from the oddball Rob Winters just described."

CHAPTER 17
BILL SNEED

Bill Sneed, manager of the busy LA Fitness Center located in Stevenson Ranch, was affable and a pleasant surprise for the two detectives. More accustomed to being greeted in an unfriendly manner, Phelps and Rich found Sneed talkative and outgoing. Best of all, he provided a wealth of information.

Carefully, the two detectives explained they were investigating the murder of Will Preston and hoped manager Sneed could assist them.

"We've studied Mr. Preston's phone and checkbooks, going back a few years, and learned he had a membership in your gym," Steven Rich volunteered. "Is there anything you can tell us about his association with your facility?" he questioned.

Sneed ushered the cops into his small office at the rear of the building. The room was overstuffed with workout equipment, brochures, advertising flyers, and announcements for fitness competitions for beginning to advanced athletes.

The floor was lined with boxes holding free weights, boxing gloves, and Dyna-Bands. Photos of several club members using various workout equipment lined the walls. Sneed opened a desk drawer and rummaged around, looking through a pile of files. Finally, he turned to his computer records.

"Oh sure, I remember Will. What a shame, he was a really nice guy. You say you got our gym number from Will's phonebook? What happened, do you have any clues?" he asked.

"We're just here to get some background info on his habits and friendships. Was he well-liked, did he have any problems or disagreements with other club members?" Roberta Phelps casually asked this, with a slight smile.

"Not that I can recall. He was just a nice guy who was here regularly, really fit, and he took his health and fitness seriously."

It was at this point in the conversation Steven Rich introduced the particulars he and Roberta Phelps had learned from their interview with Rob Winters. "Did Will Preston have any special workout partners or a personal trainer?" he asked.

"Let me check." Bill Sneed scrolled down and read the notes on his computer file. "Yeah, he was a client of Jason's, but that was a few years ago. Jason's one of our trainers," Sneed reported.

"We'd like his full name and contacts," Roberta requested. "Is there anything more you can tell us about him?"

"Name's Jason Montgomery. He's a good trainer and well-credentialed. He has all the right certifications needed. A few of our members think he's kind of an oddball, sometimes angry, but I think he's harmless. Periodically members ask for a personal trainer and Jason's one of the trainers I frequently refer members to. Some like him, others not so much." Sneed carefully copied Jason Montgomery's name, address, and phone number on a small slip of paper and handed it to Roberta.

Roberta paused from her note-taking and studied the slip of paper before asking one more question.

"Bill, are there any other club members you hooked up with Jason Montgomery, and were there any complaints?"

Once again Bill Sneed scrolled through his computerized accounts. "Oh, here's one. Quite a few years ago. He was a beginner, overweight, and out of shape. As I recall he did a bit of cardiac rehab and wanted a trainer but didn't continue with him for very long. A lot of guys start out thinking they'll stick with it, then quit. Just like the folks who make a New Year's resolution at the first of the year, but by February they're gone."

"His name please."

"Al Sanchez and here's his phone number." Sneed wrote it down on a post-it and handed it to Roberta.

Hearing the name Al Sanchez had an immediate impact on both officers. Roberta thought her heart would stop and Steven Rich caught his breath. Neither showed any outward hint of recognition but both knew Al Sanchez was a victim in one of the cold case murders they had been looking into. Here was a big red flag connecting two murder victims to the same personal trainer.

Sanchez had been killed a few years earlier and there was little to go on at the time of his death. Considered an isolated case, his murder received scant press coverage other than a local crime report and his brief obituary. Eventually, his death made its way into the cold case files and hadn't received much attention until Julia Horner and Sam Malloy suggested exercise programs and fitness club memberships might link the victims to their murderer. Phelps and Rich were now exceedingly anxious to talk to Jason Montgomery.

Hoping to gain an additional link, Steven Rich asked the club manager if Susan Jeffreys had a club membership. Once more, Bill Sneed turned to his computer screen. "No, doesn't ring a bell and she's not on our membership list."

After thanking Bill Sneed for his time and input the detectives sat in their car and planned their next steps. Both wanted to meet with Jason Montgomery as soon as possible but before doing so it was necessary to review the facts they knew. Both Sanchez and Preston were Montgomery's clients, both had been murdered with the same 9mm handgun, both crimes were committed during the mid-morning hours, and neither crime provided any clues or evidence other than the bullets removed from the victims' bodies.

Detective Rich also noted that both Bill Sneed, the health club manager, and Rob Winters described Montgomery as angry or an oddball.

Planning their questioning strategy Phelps and Rich decided to approach Montgomery in a non-threatening, non-accusatory manner. They'd present themselves as only seeking information about the victims. They'd tell him they knew he had trained both Sanchez and Preston and express gratitude for any insight he could provide. Satisfied their approach was right, they headed out in the direction of Montgomery's apartment.

Roberta had another thought. She smiled as she turned toward her partner who was in the driver's seat. "Rich, let's ask if he trained Susan Jeffreys. If he did, that'll be number three. I think we've almost got this all tied up. At least, I believe we're really close."

Steven Rich smiled and shook his head in agreement. Unfortunately, neither of them understood how far they were from being really close.

CHAPTER 18
THE BEST LAID PLANS

Since his meeting with Rob Winters at the Coffee Bean and Tea Leaf, Jason Montgomery was a mess. Never one to organize his thoughts or plan well, Jason was at a loss concerning what his next move should be regarding Rob Winters' demise.

Knowing this about himself, Jason scoffed at this limitation. He reasoned his faulty ability to plan ahead could be understood and was counter-balanced, by his extreme caution and meticulous execution of each murder he committed. He had a special talent for efficiently committing the crime once he had wrestled with the decision and concluded it was necessary to eliminate the victim.

But this situation was different and presented unusual considerations. Alive, Rob Winters could ask too many questions of him or the cops. Dead, Rob Winter's murder could lead the cops to Jason. If Jason killed Rob Winters, it might take the cops only a few months to follow a trail from Rob Winters to Bill Sneed at the LA Fitness Center, and then to Jason.

After consuming quite a lot of booze and smoking a dozen cigarettes, Jason made his decision. He would kill Winters and eliminate the possibility that Winters could link him to Will Preston. "Shit!" he yelled, bemoaning the fact that, Will Preston, had given Jason's contact information to Winters.

Because of the association with these two men, Jason reasoned this murder, unlike the others, needed to look like an accident or suicide. He didn't like this deviation from what he considered his chosen approach, but it was necessary.

Having made his decision, Jason began to relax. He was sorry he had allowed time to elapse since his meeting with Winters at the Coffee Bean and Tea Leaf, but now he finally had a plan and would hammer out the details quickly. Perhaps a hit-and-run accident was the way to go. Another possible solution was to set up another meeting with Winters and drop some poison in Winters' drink. No, he concluded, neither would look like an accident nor a suicide. He'd need to give this task some serious thought.

Settling in his desk chair Jason booted up his computer planning to research some methods that might help him devise a strategy. A knock at the door interrupted his concentration.

Angered by the disturbance, Jason's mood changed swiftly. Who the hell is going to bother me now, he thought? He needed to get work done and just as he was about to find a solution to his quandary, his attention was diverted. Jason slowly crossed the room and opened the door.

Detectives Roberta Phelps and Steven Rich introduced themselves to the open-mouthed Jason Montgomery who nervously asked, "What do ya want? I'm busy."

"We're sorry to interrupt your work but hope you can spare a few minutes. Can we come in?" Roberta asked.

"Well, okay, but make it fast. I'm really busy. What's this about?"

"We hope you can help us. We understand you knew Will Preston and Al Sanchez. We're investigating their deaths and are looking for information about them and their habits. We're talking to all their friends and family and hope to get some assistance that might provide further direction into our investigation." Steven Rich said this with a friendly smile and warm voice.

It was immediately apparent to both cops that Jason Montgomery was shaken by this news. Montgomery almost stumbled into his chair.

"Who? Who's death?" Jason asked.

"Preston and Sanchez. We think you knew both men from an affiliation with a gym you're associated with. We're talking to gym members and employees to get a handle on the activities of both victims," Roberta explained. "Is there anything you can tell us about either man?"

"I'm not a suspect, am I? I hardly knew them."

"No. We're talking to everybody who knew both men and want to eliminate you as well as many of the others we're talking to. Is there anything you can help us with?"

"Not really. I think I knew them, but I'm really busy and have a lot of clients. When I'm in the gym even people who aren't my clients ask my advice and want me to show them how to use some of the equipment. I interact with a lot of guys. The names are familiar, but I haven't seen them in years. I don't remember either of them well, so I can't help you much. You should speak to the other trainers."

"We will," Roberta answered. "Thank you for your time. If you think of anything, please give us a call. Here are our cards. Oh, one more question. Do you know Susan Jeffreys?"

"Who?" Jason's face paled and his voice quivered.

"Susan Jeffreys," Detective Rich repeated. Did you ever work out with her?"

"No, can't say I did," Jason lied. "The name means nothing to me. Now, I've got to get to work. If I think of anything, I'll let you know," he said leading them to the door.

Alone again, Jason was near panic. Desperately trying to clear his head he sat in his desk chair and struggled to gain composure. His self-talk echoed in the room as he spoke out loud. "I'm smarter than they are. They've got nothing. The dumb asses are on a fucking fishing expedition."

Swallowing hard, Jason continued his self-talk monologue. "So, I trained the two stiffs. Means nothing. I trained a lot of losers who are still walking around taking up space. Just 'cause I trained those two dummies doesn't prove a thing."

As Jason continued to talk, he could feel his pulse slow, and his heartbeat return to normal. The visit from the police, he reasoned, was just a blip in time that would lead to a dead end.

"That lucky bastard, Rob Winters, just had his life saved. No way can I get rid of him now. Better to back off. If Winters spills his guts to the cops, he'll only tell them what they already know that I was acquainted with Sanchez and Preston. No big deal, nothing to get excited about. They don't have a clue."

CHAPTER 19
PERSON OF INTEREST

The meeting was scheduled to start at 2:00 p.m. Julia Horner enjoyed her status as a full and valued member of what the precinct was now calling "the team", consisting of Detectives Roberta Phelps, Steven Rich, and retired Detective Sam Malloy, and Julia. The four of them were frequently seen engrossed in conversation with their heads buried in their note pads. Meeting in a small conference room, the four of them were a well-established smooth working group accepted by the other cops who viewed "the team's" work as important.

Julia's position on "the team" was welcomed and her judgment and sharp insight were respected. She interacted with many of the police officers, provided feedback when asked, and although an unofficial member, she had become a productive resource. Her suggestion that they examine the links between the murdered victims and various fitness activities was regarded by the police brass as a real breakthrough.

Agreeing that these unsolved crimes were committed by one serial killer, these murders, now referred to as The Mid-Morning Murders finally were being investigated as pieces of a larger puzzle. Julia was credited with that realization.

Roberta and Steven had given Sam and Julia a detailed report on their meeting with Jason Montgomery. Both detectives were sure he was the killer they were looking for. Their descriptions of Montgomery's responses, behavior, and demeanor had convinced them he was their man. Their instinct and experience had kicked in their confidence that Montgomery's behavior was that of a guilty man. They just needed to prove it.

"Right," Julia mused. "We have a person of interest, but no conclusive evidence." Her three listeners nodded their heads in agreement.

Steven summed up what they already knew. Montgomery trained both Sanchez and Preston. That was easily confirmed by the health club's records.

Roberta continued, "We've also interviewed Stan Jeffreys, Susan Jeffreys' husband, hoping to connect Montgomery to her, but had no luck there. Jeffreys told us Susan had a trainer a number of years ago, but he couldn't remember his name. He thought it was something like Jake, or Jeff, or maybe Jeremy, but he just wasn't sure. The poor guy is at a loss and is still grieving."

"Did you look at Jeffreys' records, their old checkbooks?" Sam asked.

"We asked about that, Steven responded. "Jeffreys said his wife had many talents, but balancing their checkbook wasn't one of them. According to him, his wife paid cash whenever possible and he's sure she would have paid a trainer that way."

Picking up that thread, Roberta continued, "So, we can't prove Montgomery knew the Jeffreys victim." She heaved a deep sigh and shook her head. "I know Montgomery was lying when he told us he didn't know Susan Jeffreys, but there's no way we can connect him to her."

With a sardonic laugh, Steven added, "Yeah, when we asked Montgomery if he knew Susan Jeffreys, he turned white and could hardly breathe. For sure, that dirtbag was lying."

"All this is circumstantial," Sam Malloy announced. Until we have more, Montgomery is only a person of interest. We can't consider him anything more until we have some proof. Right now, all we have is bupkis." Sam paused for a minute and thought. "Do we have enough for a search warrant? Has anyone looked for the gun?"

Both detectives shook their heads no. Roberta explained, "We've taken all we have to the Deputy Chief of the Major Crimes Division, and it's also been discussed with the Lieutenant of the Detective Bureau, but the consensus is, we need more. Our gut feelings and experiences carry weight, but to go any further, we need some hard evidence to prove what's still only a theory.

Listening to this back-and-forth discussion, Julia was beginning to feel increasing anxiety, a vague feeling of déjà vu. This reawakened her memory of her own experience with Sam Malloy, years ago. Her own victimization, her unsolved rape case, was swept aside due to the lack of evidence, not the lack of a suspect. Jason Montgomery was not even called a suspect; he was only a person of interest.

Swallowing hard, Julia interrupted. "How about using an undercover cop as bait. He could pose as someone who's looking to hire a trainer," she suggested.

Almost in unison, the detectives said no. "It's way too early and much too risky for anything like that." Roberta gently told Julia. "We'd need much more proof before anything undercover would be approved. We can't risk an officer on a hunch."

"Yeah," Rich explained. The brass would need to approve that kind of undercover operation and that's not likely to happen." The best we can hope for now is another visit to Jason Montgomery and perhaps we can scare him enough to make a mistake. We just have to continue the investigation and keep our fingers crossed that something comes out of the woodwork."

Accepting the truth that this investigation was still in its infancy, Julia closed her eyes and silently made a vow. She would give it time, she would work with the police to find clues, but she would not, could not, allow another miscarriage of justice. If the police were unable to close this case, if they were unable to find positive proof, if they couldn't collect evidence, somehow she would.

CHAPTER 20
THE POKER GAME

Sam Malloy hummed a happy tune as he readied the dining room for his six poker-playing pals due to arrive shortly. Tuesday nights were regular get-togethers when the group shared cards, gossip, snacks, and a few beers. He appreciated the company of his friends and found their time together relaxing. It gave him a chance to catch up with the comings and goings of his cronies. He was closest to his friend, Hank Morrow, the manager of a local CVS Pharmacy, but Sam enjoyed a warm friendship with each of the other group members as well.

Tom LaMonaco, the best player, was also a retired cop. Jimmy Jones, a retired car salesman, was considered a fun-loving novice at cards. The chit-chat of the group was high-intensity laughter and teasing and the financial stakes were low. They were all there to have fun, not make money.

As the games progressed and the beers were consumed, Hank frowned. Turning toward Sam, he asked for some advice.

"Who should I call to tow away an abandoned car that's been in my CVS parking lot for more than two weeks?" He asked. "It's a real eye score and I want to get it removed as soon as possible." Hank was sure Sam could provide an answer that wouldn't cost him any money.

Sam responded while surveying his hand. "Any towing company could do it. Just Google one and I know they'll be happy to accommodate." While peering over his cards, Sam looked quizzically at Hank. "Call any one of them in the morning and they'll be there by noon."

"Yeah, but I don't want them to charge me a bundle for the tow. They should charge the owner, not me," Hank reasoned.

"Who's the owner?"

"Beats me. I told you, the car's been abandoned."

"Ya' know what, I need some toothpaste, shaving cream, and some other odds and ends. I'll come over tomorrow morning to pick up a few things and I'll take a look at the car while I'm there. Maybe we can find out who owns it."

"Oh gee, thanks, Sam. That would be great," Hank smiled. On Wednesday morning Sam and Hank approached the abandoned car that was parked at the far end of the CVS lot. Circling the vehicle, Sam took out his cell phone and grabbed a picture of the license plate number. Within minutes he emailed the photo and a short message to an old friend and colleague requesting info about who the car was registered to.

Hank was amazed. "I knew you were the one to ask for help. You have more contacts than I know how to count. If I called DMV asking for that info, they'd tell me to get lost."

Sam laughed, "Well, he's not at the DMV but he'll be able to get the name easily enough. Us cops have a way of digging up what we need," he chuckled.

Next, Sam tried the driver's side door, and to his surprise, the door opened. "Well, hello there," he whispered as he slid in behind the wheel. "Hank, open the glove box and see if the registration's in there."

"Yup, I got it," Hank reported. "Looks like the owner planned to return to the car. Nobody abandons a car with their ID and registration still in it. Says here, the car belongs to a Richard Stein, here's his address."

Looking around, Sam picked up a piece of paper, left on top of the dashboard. Downloaded and printed from an online map, the paper provided driving directions to Vasquez Rocks. Sprawled across the top of the sheet was the handwritten note: "meet Jason at CVS at 10:00." Detective Malloy smiled and took a photo of the note.

Although retired, Sam Malloy immediately grasped the significance of this discovery. His cop's nose, even now, could sniff out and understand the link from this car to Jason Montgomery, the Person of Interest. But where was Richard Stein and why was his car here in the CVS Pharmacy parking lot?

Chapter 21
RELAXATION AND WORRY

"Stop! You're hurting me. Stop pushing me," she yelled. He came close to her face and screamed at her, "It's your fault and you deserved it."

The two of them stood facing each other and the shouts and threats grew in volume. Both of them were fighting mad and could not contain their fury.

Julia rushed into the room. "That's enough, both of you. Now take a deep breath and calm down. What's this all about?" she asked.

"Mom, it's his fault. He started it," Hillary cried.

"No way," was the emphatic response from her twin brother, Bobby. Shaking and pointing a finger at his sister, he continued, "She knocked the paint over and made it spill on the floor. She did it."

Separating both of them, Julia gently put an arm around each and tried to quiet the still simmering children. "Look, accidents happen.

That's why your dad and I furnished the playroom with washable and wipeable stuff. We can clean the floor and there'll be no damage to anything. As a matter of fact, you'll both clean the floor, and I don't want to hear anything more about whose fault it is." Julia's patience for this situation was spent.

Both children frowned. "Aw, Mom. But..."

Julia cut them off. "Enough! And there's no reason to get so angry and push each other around. That's no way to behave. Now make up, forgive each other, and start cleaning up. Dinner's almost ready."

"Oh God, kids!" she thought as she returned to the kitchen. "I'm too tired to deal with this."

It had been a long hard week, but Julia planned to review the events with Matt and a calming glass of wine just as soon as the dinner dishes were put away.

Often, during the quiet hours of the evening, after the kids were in bed, Julia and Matt would sit down and talk. She loved this peaceful time when they could relax and share their stories, their hopes, their dreams. It was always a welcome time when they could renew and reconnect, momentarily free of the stress of work and responsibility. These special times alone together were treasures. But lately, the topic uppermost in both their minds was the Mid-Morning Murder case.

"So, what's happening at the office?" Matt queried. He asked this, partly to soothe Julia, but also because he was interested to know what kept her so busy. He waited a short time before Julia was ready to answer.

"Nothing really, same old, same old," Julia reported. "I'm more concerned with what's happening with the LA Police. It seems to me there's an awful lot of foot-dragging. It's been weeks since our Person of Interest was identified, and nothing has progressed since then."

"Aren't they following up on any leads?" Matt asked.

"There aren't that many to go on. I know detectives Phelps and Rich are poking around, and I trust their experience and judgment, but for the life of me, I wish things were moving along faster."

"Well, what have they been doing?"

Taking a swallow of her wine Julia flatly reported they were still interviewing people, leading only to more dead ends. She shook her head in dismay and took another sip from her wine glass.

"I'm sure they know what they're doing. These things do take time. It's only on TV that it's wrapped up in an hour."

Julia's face expressed worry. "They haven't found a gun; they still have no evidence. Rich and Phelps returned to the Person of Interest's apartment and searched it. They were able to convince the powers that be to give them a search warrant, but it produced nothing usable. It just seems like they are so far from finding the truth.

"Julia don't make yourself sick over this. You've helped them as much as possible. If this is too much for you, withdraw from your involvement. You're not joined to the LAPD at the hip."

Matt read the worry on Julia's face. Trying to console her, he continued, "Look, you're a brilliant lawyer, a fabulous wife, and mother, you do more and care more about people than anyone else I know. Cut yourself some slack. You don't need to become the next Agatha Christie."

Julia smiled warmly hearing his praise and really appreciated his high regard. Nevertheless, Julia was experiencing fear. Fear for the future, for her children, fear for a society that seemed unable to right the wrongs that plagued so many individuals and communities. If it was within her power to bring about change, to protect those who were unable to protect themselves, if she could safeguard and shield others from harm, she felt duty-bound to do so.

"No, Matt. I can't withdraw my involvement. That's not what I want. If anything, I am willing to work harder and see how I can help more."

"Honey," Matt lowered his voice. "I don't want you working harder. You've already provided enormous assistance to the police, and I know they appreciate your input." Matt hugged her and together they snuggled comfortably in each other's arms.

That night, their lovemaking was both passionate and tender. They fell asleep embracing, each lulled by the warmth and joy of their happiness and contentment.

Sometime after midnight, Julia awakened with a start. Her heart was racing, and her mind was in turmoil. A dark realization suddenly gripped her conscious thoughts. Julia measured Matt's earlier words and she understood her value to the police. Viewed as a professional and respected, Julia functioned as an insider, yet she was not "out in the field." Julia's contribution was akin to being in a desk job. What she provided was solid information. Although, mixed with her feeling of pride was a pronounced feeling of frustration that it was leading nowhere.

Identifying a Person of Interest was a giant step forward that abruptly ended. Now, after months of questions with no solutions in sight, something more had to be done. With trepidation, Julia began to toy with the idea that trapping the murderer somehow might be the only way. And that it might become her task alone.

CHAPTER 22
SETTING A TRAP

Sam Malloy's discovery and report of the abandoned car left in the CVS parking lot pointed to Jason Montgomery as the killer responsible for the Mid-Morning. Murders. All involved in solving the case were sure Montgomery was their man but none of the cops felt there was enough evidence to convince a jury. All the evidence collected so far was circumstantial; they had found no smoking gun.

In the three weeks since the identity of the car's owner was confirmed, and a missing person report filed on Dick Stein, the investigation inched forward. Friends and coworkers of Stein's filed the report and the victim's apartment had been searched. The driving directions to Vazquez Rocks, found in Stein's car, prompted an intensive search for Stein's body, which was found early last week. The autopsy revealed the bullet that killed Stein came from the same weapon used in the other Mid-Morning Murders.

The lead detectives, as well as Sam Malloy and Julia, were frustrated. Believing they found the murderer was bitter-sweet. Through tireless work, months of pounding the pavement, and talking to scores of people who knew the victims and/or the suspect, they concluded they had found the killer. Finding direct evidence to clinch the case and get a guilty verdict was quite another challenge. For the time being, Montgomery remained a Person of Interest and nothing more.

Meeting frequently during the past weeks, Julia and Malloy's disappointment and irritation grew. On the one hand, they understood the necessity of doing everything possible to satisfy the DA's demands that direct evidence was needed for a conviction, but on the other hand, the slow pace and delays made it more likely there might be more deaths at Montgomery's hands.

Malloy joined Julia for coffee and bagels on a bright Saturday morning to brainstorm possible solutions. "Julia, I'm so irritated by the department's rules and regs, that I just might do something on my own. I'm retired now, I know the ropes, and I've been around the block more than once. On top of all that, I don't answer to a boss," Sam emphatically stated.

Julia set down her coffee mug on the end table and cupped her hands over her mouth. She took a deep breath and searched Sam's face hoping to find some clue that might indicate what he was thinking. "Sam, please don't tell me you're thinking of doing something dangerous. I know this case has gotten under your skin, but it's not your responsibility to take chances. You no longer carry a badge and you're not paid to take risks."

"Don't worry about me, Julia. This isn't my first rodeo; I know how to handle myself. I've been down this road before."

"What on earth are you thinking?" Julia's voice carried concern with a good dose of respect.

"Detectives Phelps and Rich both searched Montgomery's apartment some months ago, but not recently. I'd like to look around and see if I can find anything new. I can easily get into his apartment when he's gone. I know how to do that. I'll just nose around, see if anything turns up."

"Sam, that's against the law! You'd be entering illegally," Julia gasped.

Sam issued a deep belly laugh and doubled over. "Julia, that's why I love you. You're such an innocent, so pure. I wish I had a dime for every time I've entered a perp's place. Trust me, I know what I'm doing.

"If you insist that you must do this, how will you know when Montgomery's gone or for how long he'll be away from home?" she asked. Her voice expressed deep concern.

"Not a problem. I can stake out his place and follow his schedule, see where he goes and for how long he's gone. I'm sure that will be the easy part," Sam assured her.

After considerable discussion, the two colleagues said goodbye, but back in her office, Julia sat at her desk methodically analyzing various options. Should she accompany Sam in his quest for evidence? No, that would be illegal, and she could be disbarred for that infraction.

Should she ask Detectives Phelps and Rich to conduct another search and prevent Sam from doing so himself? No, they would not be granted another warrant without additional information. Should she do nothing? No!

No, Julia reasoned, it wasn't fair to allow Sam to take all the risk. In a strange and unofficial way, she and Sam had become partners; partners who were determined to pick up the slack and circumvent the barriers created by bureaucratic rules and regulations. It was now up to the two of them to get the direct evidence needed.

Julia paced the floor imagining several scenarios that might yield information from Montgomery. Finally, she had a plan; get him to become her personal trainer. But under no circumstances could she allow Montgomery to learn her real name or where she lived. Convinced she needed to invent a new identity, Julia decided to create a phantom persona with an assumed name and life history.

"Name, name, I need a new name," she murmured aloud. "Barbara, I like the name,

Barbara. Yes, I'll be Barbara Rumsfeld. That sounds good."

   Closing her eyes, and whispering a silent prayer, Julia located her cell phone and made a call. She swallowed hard and said, "Hello Mr. Montgomery, my name is Barbara Rumsfeld and I'd like to meet with you. I want to hire a personal trainer."

CHAPTER 23
PERSON OF INTELLECT

Roberta Phelps and Steven Rich visited Jason's apartment a second time and repeated the questions they had previously asked. They hoped to catch him with conflicting answers, but his story remained unchanged. His demeanor revealed anger and contempt and he was pretty close-mouthed, providing few details and limited information.

"Why are you here again?" Jason demanded. "I already told you as much as I know." This question, asked by Jason, was a defiant rebuke of authority and he sullenly folded his arms across his chest. Leaning closer into the cops' personal space, he almost hissed as he spoke.

Both detectives noticed but were not dissuaded by his hostile attitude. Confident they would eventually arrest him they tolerated his antagonistic behavior, grateful that they weren't being greeted by a waving gun. As experienced interviewers, they were able to ignore his aggression and continued to calmly question him.

"Mr. Montgomery," Phelps smiled, "You can answer our questions here or downtown. What location would you prefer?" She sternly asked with a hint of sarcasm.

Frowning, Jason reluctantly answered their inquires in terse sentences and was relieved when they finally left.

Almost immediately he realized they considered him a person of interest and his initial reaction was fear. He paced the floor silently cursing, but within minutes, his impaired reasoning once again kicked in and began to change his view of the situation.

"Damned friggin' cops. Who the hell do they think they're talking to? I'm not some lowlife they can push around and intimidate. I shoulda thrown them out."

His strong belief in his infallibility countered reality. Jason's mental disorder permitted him to justify his behaviors as appropriate and convinced him he was blameless. Sure of his intellect and wisdom, Jason reviewed everything that had transpired between himself and the two police officers. He was certain they had nothing and were only on a repeated fishing expedition.

Believing his murderous actions rested upon legitimate decisions, Jason's fear and concern ultimately evaporated, leaving him feeling safe and supercilious.

"I am a person of intellect," he boldly proclaimed. "Those fools may refer to me as a person of interest, but they are wrong!" His voice grew louder as he again, proclaimed, "I AM A PERSON of INTELLECT."

A manic burst of euphoria propelled Jason to shadow box across the room thrusting first one, then the other fist, forcefully into the air. His footwork was quick, and he deftly shifted his weight as he moved about. The rhythm of his steps was carefully timed to coincide with the cadence of his shouts, "I AM A PERSON OF INTELLECT."

His rapid movements increased his pulse and heartbeat. He broke into a sweat but was enjoying this sudden burst of activity. "I'm physically fit and mentally strong!"

Jason's narcissism, his sense of entitlement, and admiration for his own abilities permitted him to snicker and dismiss the detective's veiled accusations.

Obviously, Jason reasoned, he needed to be careful going forward. He recognized his decision not to kill Rob Winters was the right call. He'd like to fuck up the twerp's life in some way, however, because he was sure it was Rob Winters' phone message, left on Will Preston's, phone, that led the cops to him. Perhaps at some time in the future, Jason would deal with Winters and give him payback for supplying his name to the police. But now was not the right time to satisfy his need for revenge.

Feeling secure, Jason reveled in his self-defined status as a "Person of Intellect" and turned his attention to his cell phone calendar. "Okay, looks like I have time to work out in the morning tomorrow, and then I've scheduled a meeting with a prospective client. Somebody named Barbara Rumsfeld. I'll see what this bimbo has to offer."

CHAPTER 24
BREAKING AND ENTERING

The lock was easy to pick. There was no alarm, no safety chain, and no barking dog. Good, he thought, and as he entered the apartment, Malloy moved swiftly and silently, heading directly to Montgomery's desk. Unsure of exactly what he was looking for Sam paused for a moment and looked around.

The apartment was non-descript. A few sports magazines cluttered the floor, and a discarded carton of milk was left on the coffee table. Dirty dishes filled the kitchen sink.

Malloy decided to rummage through the mail and papers on Montgomery's desk and then if time permitted, he'd try to see if he could find anything on Montgomery's computer. Sam was fully aware that if he found anything it could not be used as evidence at a trial because it was obtained illegally. Nevertheless, he reasoned that any incriminating information he found might influence the police to intensify their investigation and speed up this slow-moving case.

Malloy, sure he had approximately an hour and a half of uninterrupted time in Montgomery's place began searching methodically, overlooking nothing.

For several weeks Malloy had watched Jason's activities and he was confident Montgomery was now with a client.

The sound of a key in the door lock made the hair on the back of Malloy's neck stand on end. For a split second, the retired detective stood motionless as panic and concern quickened his heartbeat. Swiftly, he moved to the bedroom and crouched down behind a large upholstered easy chair in the corner of the room, hoping it was big enough to keep him out of sight. His presence might be undetected if Montgomery didn't enter the bedroom.

Sam listened intently and heard Montgomery open and then close a few desk drawers. "Shit," Montgomery whispered. "Car keys, car keys - where did I leave them?" he muttered. "I knew I shoulda put all my keys on the same chain." Montgomery's footsteps approached the bedroom.

Sam apprehensively held his breath as Montgomery entered the bedroom. He went straight for the closet and opened the door. "Keys, keys, where the fuck are my keys?" Montgomery repeated as he rifled through several pockets. Finally, he let out a victorious little yelp, waved the keys in the air, and left!

Exiting from his hiding place, Sam thanked his lucky stars he hadn't tried to hide inside the closet! Collecting his thoughts and calm once again, Sam returned to Jason's desk and the stack of papers. Studying one specific bill Sam issued a slow whistle.

"Well, well, well. Looky here." Sam took out his cell phone and took a photo of the bill. The bill, addressed to Jason Montgomery, was from Gill's Guns and Ammo shop, and documented the purchase of bullets for a 9mm gun, as well as rental time at the shooting range. Also included on the bill of sale was the purchase of a silencer. It clearly established Jason's access to ammunition and his familiarity with guns.

Sam was careful to replace the bill where he found it within the packet of bills. Leaving the apartment, he made sure he left no sign of his entry. He couldn't wait to share his discovery with Julia, and Detectives Phelps and Rich.

CHAPTER 25
CHUTZPAH

Julia marveled at her courage and chutzpah. These feelings were coupled with a fair dose of apprehension that quickly expanded to fear. She and Jason Montgomery scheduled their meeting at a small local coffee shop, a very public location, and Julia sat at a central booth awaiting Jason Montgomery's arrival. As she waited, Julia reviewed her simple plan. She would explain she visited his website, reviewed his qualifications, and decided that he appeared to be just the trainer to help her begin an exercise program.

Julia would tell him there was no need to shop around, she liked what he wrote about his approach and goals and wanted to schedule workout sessions as soon as possible. As she continued to wait, she hoped her explanation would signal no red flags and she fervently prayed she could keep her composure. She had always managed to keep her cool during difficult courtroom closing arguments, but this situation carried greater risk.

Montgomery entered the small coffee shop and looked around searching the room. Recognizing him from his website photo, Julia waved a greeting. As he approached her table, she studied his appearance and demeanor. He was casually dressed, looked physically fit, as one would expect, and was well-groomed. "My God," Julia thought. "He looks like a normal person, not the murderous monster I know him to be."

Her mind raced as conflicting thoughts flooded her brain. Part of her wanted to run, yet she remained still. Another part of her wanted to strike him but she managed a welcoming smile.

Concealing her emotional turmoil, Julia managed to summon her strength hoping her voice revealed none of her apprehension or fear. She looked directly at Jason and calmly said, "Your website photo doesn't do you justice. You're much better looking," and offered him her hand to shake. She was surprised at how easily those words had flown out of her mouth.

Unexpectedly, Julia realized her first response was one of flattery and femininity. She wondered where this greeting had come from. It did not reflect her feelings or usual behavior. Successfully concealing her loathing of him, Julia realized that it was necessary to appear a complaint and docile female. She correctly surmised Montgomery would find her unthreatening. Julia's hunch was on target.

Jason accepted her compliment and did his own evaluation of this prospective client. Piece of cake, he thought. She'll be easy money and an easy lay, he reasoned.

"Thanks, honey." He gushed giving her a warm smile. "You're easy on the eyes, too." Patting her hand he asked, "Can I call you Barbara?"

Julia inwardly recoiled, but she showed no sign of hesitancy and returned his smile. The game of insincerity had begun.

"So, Barbara, sweetheart, what attracted you to my website?" he asked. Julia was momentarily stunned. "Good Lord," she thought. She had almost forgotten she had created this alias but quickly adjusted to her new identity.

"I don't know. It was one of the first I stumbled upon when I started my search and it just seemed to meet my needs." Julia answered. What a Neanderthal, she thought. Please make him stop with the honeys and sweethearts. He's clueless.

As Jason listened, he scrutinized her appearance and attitude. Since the recent visit and investigation by Detectives Rich and Phelps, Jason knew he had to be careful. Not wanting to risk taking on new clients who might become problematic, Jason realized his behavior and interactions would be closely followed by the police. He couldn't chance working with anyone who might ignite his anger or cause him to unleash his need for retribution. Jason knew when he was in a rage his impulse control was limited, and he understood he needed to protect himself from those needy folks who sparked the desire in him to eliminate them.

Believing he properly assessed Julia's truthfulness and trustworthiness, Jason relaxed a bit. He too, allowed his thoughts to wander and he imagined this new client might soon fall into bed with him.

After discussing fees, hours, and fitness goals, Jason and Julia agreed theirs was a perfect match. The deceptions and falsehoods continued, and each pretended their objectives were in sync. They agreed Julia (who he called Barbara) should join a fitness center and Jason suggested she contact Bill Sneed; manager of the LA Fitness Center located in Stevenson Ranch and get a membership application. Jason reassured her it was a good club.

The club's location was some distance from Julia's home, but she also felt this was a plus. Realizing she had to keep her true purpose, and personal safety, as secure as possible, Julia was willing to travel to keep her home life and personal relationships under wraps.

To safeguard her family Julia invented a fabricated persona, just as she had invented the false name, Barbara. And Julia carefully laid out a false backstory. Satisfied that the story she concocted was believable she was determined to play the role she designed.

Over coffee, Julia convincingly talked about her fictitious past. Her confidence and boldness increased as she told Jason she was divorced and lived alone. She painted a picture of a nasty, vengeful ex-husband who constantly tried to intimidate her. Fearful that he might break into her apartment, she had decided to work out and get stronger. She was also considering taking some self-defense classes.

This contest of lies and deceit continued as each tested the veracity of the other.

Finally, they said goodbye and confirmed their first workout session for the next Thursday morning at 11:00 a.m. She entered the time and date in her calendar with a feeling of apprehension. Steadying her resolve, Julia promised herself if she felt endangered, she'd quickly end the commitment. But above all, she hoped that would not become necessary and she would do all in her power to prevent that possibility.

Not ready to interrupt her train of thought, Julia remained in the coffee shop and reviewed her plan. She'd portray her behavior with her nonexistent ex-spouse as meek and timid. Over a period of time, she'd tell Montgomery she felt powerless, and how exhausting it was dealing with her former husband, who constantly intimidated and tried to control her. She'd ask Montgomery's advice and inquire how he dealt with difficult clients. She'd flatter his wisdom, good sense, and intelligence. She'd tell him that any suggestions he could provide about self-protection would be gratefully accepted.

Julia knew she was playing with fire and long after Jason left, she sat at the small table visibly shaking.

CHAPTER 26
BRAVERY AND TERROR

More than three weeks had elapsed since Sam Malloy's break-in at Jason Montgomery's residence. During that time period the police, Julia, and Sam met at police headquarters and discussed the case many times, posting details, photos of the victims, and lists of clues on a large evidence board, which they studied intently and sometimes hotly debated. The group vacillated, at times believing Jason worked alone and at other times arguing he had accomplices. Julia remained convinced he was the only one involved in these criminal acts and was sure the case would not be closed until and unless the police were united in their theories.

"Wait just one minute," Julia shrieked during one exchange. "There's nothing pointing to an accomplice. Why are you speculating about something without any basis? We all had agreed he worked alone."

"Calm down, Julia," Roberta admonished. "We need to explore all possibilities. If you're unhappy with our progress and policies, you can bow out of the team at any time!"

Each member of the team was experiencing stress and frustration. Periodically raw nerves hit the breaking point and angry exchanges resulted. In spite of their occasional outbursts, everyone in the group liked and respected one another. They were professionals and aware that this case was the common bond uniting them. They also knew they wanted to continue working together until the case was solved. During their ups and downs, they still had each other's back, would overlook differences, and pull together to achieve their desired goal.

The circumstantial evidence grew gradually, and Detectives Rich and Phelps generously gave their civilian colleagues full credit for the work they had put into this case. However, despite this recognition, Julia was frustrated and angered by the delay and lack of agreement.

When Sam informed Julia about his illegal entry into Montgomery's apartment she experienced a mixture of emotions. Part of her lamented Sam's illegal action. After all, Julia was a practicing lawyer, and thereby an advocate of the truth and obeying the law. But on the other hand, she was human and thought, "that fucker deserves what he gets." If this is what it takes to gain needed evidence, she was on board. For the time being, both she and Sam withheld this information from their colleagues.

Julia chuckled a bit recognizing she, too, had crossed the line by creating a false identity. And she reasoned her lies to Jason about her name and life weren't illegal and served a greater good. She could forgive these deceptions if they aided the quick apprehension and conviction of this criminal.

Sam wasn't at risk of being disbarred or demoted. As a retiree, he was free from having to worry about his professional standing. Julia, still practicing in a law firm, knew her actions had to remain within the confines of the law. Her plan, not without risk, was perfectly legal even though very dangerous.

She dared not let her colleagues know that for the last several weeks she had been exercising with Jason Montgomery and would continue to meet with him at the gym. Fearing they would, for safety reasons, insist she abandon her association with Montgomery, she had given them no hint of her involvement with him.

Exhausted from the tense meeting, later in the day, Julia savored some quiet time at home. Both Hillary and Bobbie were away on a school trip and Matt was out of town at a conference. Julia collapsed into the easy chair in her den with a glass of wine. Anticipating her next workout with Montgomery she reviewed her invented persona and carefully memorized the background on Barbara she had already shared with him.

Her relaxation was interrupted by the ringing of her new cell phone. It was the phone she recently bought, exclusively to communicate with Montgomery. She had purchased this phone to make sure he couldn't connect it to her real identity.

"Hi cutie," Jason began. "How about some fun time together after our next workout?"

"What do you have in mind? she asked apprehensively.

"I was thinking maybe lunch and then a drive to a park in Santa Clarita. Maybe we could picnic there."

"Oh my God," Julia silently gasped, not emitting a sound. Her emotions swung between feelings of bravery and terror as she silently thought, "That's where Will Preston was killed."

CHAPTER 27
THE MEETING AT THE RANGE

The sign was clearly visible in the front window: Gill's Guns and Ammo. Sam double checked the address on the bill he had copied from the papers he found on Jason's desk. He was in the right place.

Uncertain exactly what to look for, Sam just hoped he could uncover information that would help him get a feel for Jason's routines and habits by picking the brain of the shop's proprietor. Before entering the establishment, he reviewed the items listed on the bill of sale that had been issued to Jason. There was the purchase of bullets for a 9mm gun, as well as rental time at the shooting range. Also listed was the purchase of a silencer.

Since Sam's recent entry into Jason's apartment, he had been keeping track of Jason's movements as best he could. He couldn't follow the suspect on a full-time basis and certainly wasn't authorized by the police to do so. However, Sam felt he needed to keep a watchful eye on Jason Montgomery. Sam knew Jason frequently practiced target shooting at the range located at Gill's Guns and Ammo and he had reason to believe that Jason might be there today. Trying his best to look like a casual shopper he slowly walked around the place periodically looking at one item, then another.

The facility was large and bustling with patrons. The front door opened to a wide area with showcases full of handguns, carrying cases and silencers, and hundreds of boxes of ammo. A short corridor on the left led to another room filled with hunting equipment and scores of accessories used by hunters. Rows of binoculars, flashlights, gun cleaning equipment, ear protectors, and targets filled the shelves and glass-topped counters.

Another area of this large room held displays for archery enthusiasts. Bows, arrows, quivers, leather arm guards, and boxes of bowstrings filled the floor space and countertops. Several shoppers were looking at various items and checking prices. The entire establishment was filled with the scent of gun oil and cleaner.

Sam approached a young man behind the counter who was organizing and straightening the hunting display. "Hi, I hope you can help me," Sam smiled.

"Yes, sir. What can I do for you?" As he turned, Sam noticed the name "Gill" embroidered on his shirt. This young fellow was obviously the owner, just the person Sam wanted to talk to. With a broad smile, Sam started a conversation.

"A friend of mine comes here often and practices target shooting at your range. He thinks highly of your facility and the knowledge of your employees. I have a few questions."

"Shoot, no pun intended," Gill said with a chuckle.

"Do you need a membership in the club to use the range or is it possible to target shoot as a guest?" Sam asked.

"You can use the range as a guest but first you must fill out a questionnaire, show a photo ID, sign a waiver, and indicate your level of gun experience. Ya' know, all the standard pain in the butt paperwork."

"Oh, no problem, I'm a retired cop," Sam informed him. Continuing the conversation, Sam began to chat, working up to the questions that were more meaningful to him.

"I bet you see a lot of weirdos here. Any characters you think have questionable motives? Does the store have a group of regulars? You know, people who come in on a routine basis?"

"No sir, our clientele is tops. No problems here. We make sure to do all the necessary background checks before selling to people. We go by the book here," Gill said defensively.

Believing he had reached a dead-end, Sam ended the conversation, wishing he could have gotten more information. He decided he might as well take the time to get in some target practice. A clerk copied Sam's photo ID driver's license and the completed forms and placed everything in a file cabinet. The waiver and a sign-in sheet to use the shooting range were given to Sam for his signature. Gill informed him that he could use Bay Number 4, and the corridor leading to the range was on the right.

"Good timing, there's just one other shooter presently using the range and he's in Bay Number 1."

With pen in hand, Sam studied the sign-in sheet. His hunch was confirmed. Printed on the sign-in sheet, was the name of the only other shooter assigned to Bay Number 1. The name scrawled in big letters was Jason Montgomery.

Bracing for the unexpected, Sam entered the range and was greeted by the pungent smell of gun smoke and Hoppe's gun cleaner. Montgomery, the man in Bay Number 1, stood facing the target 50 feet away. The target hung suspended on a motorized track, depicting a male figure outlined in black with the typical bullseye over the heart. Montgomery stood with his legs widely set apart and both arms extended. He fired several well-aimed rounds, each grouping in the target's heart. Jason Montgomery could easily qualify as a sharpshooter.

"Nice shooting," Sam roared so that Montgomery could hear him through the ear protectors.

Montgomery turned and nodded a silent thank you and returned his attention to the target.

Carefully placing his equipment in Bay Number 4, Sam considered his next exchange. For several minutes the two men shot without conversation, Sam only occasionally making a comment, trying to establish rapport.

"Do you shoot here often?" Sam asked.

"Yeah, now and then."

"What are you shooting? Is that a 9mm?"

Jason grunted answers without revealing much. Sam resumed his efforts. "I'm thinking of buying a 9mm. Yours seems easy to handle and you certainly have good aim and control."

"Here, want to try a few rounds with it?" Jason offered.

"That would be great. You can try mine."

The two shooters exchanged weapons, each testing the accuracy of the other's ability. Eventually, each man changed the distance of their targets and set the motorized track to carry the sheets to closer or more distant points. The men became more relaxed with each other, and their banter continued.

Sam had hoped he'd find Montgomery at the range, but silently wondered how to direct the future of this meeting. The only thing Sam knew for sure was that he had to proceed with caution. If he appeared too friendly or asked too many questions, Montgomery's reaction might be unpredictable and could become dangerous. Sam was hoping he could establish some kind of relationship with Montgomery. Maybe suggest things they had in common in an attempt to build a connection or foster Montgomery's interest in becoming shooting buddies.

"Do you think I should buy a gun safe to keep my weapons in?" Sam volunteered. "This is a new hobby for me. I need a mentor to teach me the ropes. Where do you keep your gun?" Sam asked.

"Yeah, a gun safe would be a good place to keep a gun. It would be secure there," was Montgomery's non-committal response. Without another word, Jason collected his equipment, packed his unused bullets, and carefully swept up the spent bullet casings, retrieving all but one that had rolled out of sight onto the first few feet of the range. He then retrieved the target, folded it, placed it in his shooting bag, and abruptly left the range.

Sam waited, making sure Jason had exited the building, and walked the short distance to Bay Number 1. Crouching down, he removed a pen from his pocket and deftly picked up the spent cartridge Jason had overlooked. Wrapping it in a tissue, Sam gingerly pocketed the possible evidence that might hold fingerprints and unique markings.

CHAPTER 28
THE EMERGENCE OF BARBARA

"Breathe, breathe!", he shouted. "Don't stop now. Be tough," he insisted. No sissy stuff," Jason commanded. He was leaning in towards her and his face loomed over her as she struggled.

Julia sat at the leg press machine and took another gulp of air into her lungs, extended her legs, and pushed the weight as hard as possible.

"Eighteen, nineteen, twenty." Jason loudly counted down Julia's repetitions. "Glad to see at least you're trying," he said.

The movement and din of chatter in the gym stopped as Jason's voice and orders filled the room. Several of those who were exercising stopped and stared at them. Jason's voice and outbursts were familiar to the regulars who routinely frequented the gym.

Their workout sessions were intense, and Julia was pushed to her limit. Each time they met, Jason increased the difficulty and presented new challenges. Always active, Julia was strong and fit, but Jason devised new drills and aerobic activities that were more demanding with each session. Determined not to give in, she pushed herself hard. But she also wondered if Jason was this demanding of all his clients or whether he had singled her out for punishment.

Julia reasoned there was no way she would give up or give in. She'd continue working out with Jason until she had what she needed. And that was information, some clues, or a way to find some closure to the case. He was guilty of many crimes. She knew it, and she'd find a way to prove it.

Despite her fear of him, her loathing of spending time with him, she had to admit these workout sessions were making her stronger. Perhaps this was an added benefit in addition to her goal of learning more about him and his behaviors.

They'd been meeting at the gym regularly during the last several weeks. Sometimes Jason appeared relaxed and conversant and at other times he was dictatorial, demanding, and rude. It was easy for Julia to understand that Jason's mood swings could be off-putting to many. She was sure some of his clients would opt out and either switch to other trainers or abandon fitness activities altogether. She vowed there was no way she'd go that route. She'd put up with him no matter what.

Julia always paid close attention to Jason's mood swings. On days when he was more approachable, she talked about her nonexistent ex-husband, pretending to fear him, in order to reinforce what she wanted Jason to believe. Over the last few meetings with Jason, she had expanded this fable, telling Jason she was sure her former husband meant to do her harm and cheat her out of what was rightfully hers. Hesitant to provide too much detail, Julia only dropped small bits of her web of deceit at a time. She decided to drop another kernel today.

"You know, we had a nice summer cabin in the mountains where we would enjoy holidays and weekends," she lied. "The divorce settlement granted me ownership of the cabin and it's totally mine. He owns no part of it, but boy, he'll do anything to get his grubby hands on it."

They had finished their workout session and were seated at the juice bar, located near the entrance to the fitness center.

"Yeah?" Jason grunted. "Is it a nice place? Do you go there a lot?"

"It's a very nice place but I don't go often because I'm afraid he'll show up. I need to figure out how to get him to leave me alone. Maybe he'll find another girlfriend," Julia said wistfully.

Jason stretched his arms out and took a long swig of his juice. He said nothing for a few minutes and then frowned. "I have an older sister named Alice. She lives in Las Vegas, and she has similar problems with her ex-husband, just like you do." Taking another drink from his juice bottle, Jason continued his story. "Her ex is a real bully, and he tries to muscle her for money whenever he can. The guy's a pest and lowlife but I told Alice how to put a stop to his demands. I told her to get a gun for protection. A gun would frighten him off. You should do the same," he advised.

"No. I'm too chicken to do that," she answered. "Are you and Alice close?" she asked.

"Not so much anymore. We used to be tight. Now our relationship is hit or miss, but both of us understand that in a pinch, we'd have each other's back."

Julia listened quietly as Jason continued. "Alice is some kind of dealer or pit boss or something in one of those fancy casinos. Maybe she's only a hostess, but she seems to like it there. I don't know, but I still think she needs a gun."

Jason became serious. "Look, Barbara, if anything happened, and your ex increased the pressure, you'd need to show him you're the boss. If he became violent and you needed to use a gun for protection, it would be self-defense."

Once again, Julia bridled at being called Barbara, her assumed and still unfamiliar name. She quickly stifled her surprise and shook her head, no. "I'm just gonna keep the deed to the place locked up in my desk until I figure out what to do." She let that fallacy sit there without any further explanation.

"You have it locked in your desk? At your place?" he asked. "Well, that's dumb. If he breaks in, the first place he'd look for stuff would be your desk. You need a better place to stash things you don't want to be found."

"Yeah? Like where? I can't keep it in the cabin, he'd find it there. Should I keep it in a safe deposit box in a bank?" she asked.

"No, because he could find the key, and also if you need to get to the stuff fast, and the bank's closed, you're out of luck. Put it, and any other stuff you might need fast someplace only you would look and have access to. I'd hide stuff where I work. He won't be allowed into your place of employment and wouldn't be able to get in and rummage around."

"Oh, good idea," she said and smiled.

CHAPTER 29
A BREAKTHROUGH

Believing she found a breakthrough that might lead to proving Jason's guilt, Julia thought over her newly acquired information. Again, and again Julia mentally repeated Jason's words. *"I'd hide stuff where I work. Your ex won't go to your place of employment, and he wouldn't be able to get in and rummage around."*

Julia was sure she had uncovered a vital clue that could lead to locating the missing gun used in all the unsolved murders. She was convinced the murder weapon was hidden somewhere in the gym most often used by Jason.

She also realized finding the gun was a problem that needed to be addressed legally and by the authorities. It was unrealistic to think she could conduct an unobserved search on her own and even if she found anything it would be gained illegally and therefore would be inadmissible in a court of law. Julia spent many sleepless nights wondering how to proceed.

There was no denying the fact that Julia had to discuss this new info with Sam. Together they'd figure out how to move forward. She was reluctant to tell him, or anyone else, that she had employed Jason as her trainer: that they were meeting frequently and building a relationship. Julia sensed Sam would be horrified by the realization that she was repeatedly exposing herself to the danger of spending time with Jason Montgomery. Nevertheless, Julia knew she had to bring Sam into the loop and face his disapproval. She smiled at the thought of Sam's protective feelings even while anticipating his objections.

With a mixture of reluctance and expectancy, Julia called Sam and asked if she could drive over and meet with him. "I have information that I need to discuss with you in person. I'm on my way over to the cottage and will be there shortly."

Once on the road, Julia's mind retraced her friendship with Sam. She marveled at how their once hostile relationship had developed into a warm friendship and close comradery. She shook her head remembering the time when she, a crime victim, sought Sam's sympathy and the swift apprehension of her attacker, but only found his doubtfulness and uncertainty.

"Life takes some amazing turns," she mused. The cop she once feared and hated for his apparent reluctance to help turned out to be a giving supportive friend who just goes by the book and tries to negotiate what, at times, seem to be unavoidable stumbling blocks.

Even Julia's husband, Matt, enjoyed Sam's friendship and grew to understand the constraints Sam had to deal with while actively on the police force. The two men got along well, and the past bitterness had dissipated long ago. Matt, like Julia, now understood that while Sam was a working detective, he had to use what leads he had, leave no stone unturned, and find evidence. Without hard proof, documentation, or substantiation, cases go into the cold case file.

Julia had been to Sam's cottage previously and knew the way. As she arrived, she was greeted enthusiastically by Maisie who wagged her tail excitedly. She playfully scratched Maisie's head as she entered the living room and sat down opposite Sam.

"Sam", she started on a positive note, "I have some good news."

"What's that?" he asked, his curiosity peaked.

"I may have a lead on where Jason has hidden the murder weapon."

"Wow! How on earth could you have come by that news? Where'd you get the lead?"

"Jason told me." She almost whispered.

Sam's head jerked around, and he stared at her in disbelief. "What! What were you doing talking to him? Have you seen him? He doesn't even know you." Sam hastily added.

"Wait, one question at a time," Julia cautioned. "I'll start at the beginning." She took a breath expecting Sam to raise even more questions.

"First, I want to tell you he does not know who I am. I'm perfectly safe and I've taken no chances." Although reporting these safeguards,

Julia noticed the worry on Sam's face was not diminished.

She continued, "Again, he has no idea who I am. He thinks I'm just another client."

Sam exploded! "Are you crazy, Julia? Please don't tell me you've been meeting with him," he pleaded.

"Well, he thinks my name is Barbara. I've been extremely careful. I use a disposable phone when we talk, and I've invented a false identity. He thinks I'm a divorcee. Really, Sam, I've taken all the necessary precautions."

Sam rose to his feet and started pacing the room. "Julia, I can't believe you've taken this risk. He's a very dangerous man. I want you to stop this immediately."

For the next two hours, Sam shot numerous questions at Julia, and she provided what she thought were reassuring answers. She retold Sam many of her conversations with Jason and explained in detail that she had portrayed herself as a divorced woman afraid of an abusive ex-husband. Her explanations seemed to have little effect.

Describing her tale of keeping the deed to a nonexistent cabin in her desk drawer, Julia hoped Sam would understand that Jason accepted the scenario as true. "And that's when he told me to move the deed out of my desk and hide it someplace where I work," Julia explained.

Sam and Julia repeated each conversation, pulled apart every bit of the fabrication, debated all the assumptions, and reviewed it all again and again. Julia was adamant, she would not stop the charade and insisted her association with Jason was essential to finding proof of his guilt.

Sam reluctantly agreed, but only after extracting the promise that Julia would report to Sam all of her dates, movements, and activities with Jason, and let him know in advance where she would be going with him.

Negotiations between the two continued with Sam repeatedly insisting they inform Detectives Rich and Phelps about Julia's new and dangerous connection with Jason. Julia was enraged by

Sam's demand. Their battle of strategy heightened.

"I can handle this," she argued. "I won't take any risks. We work out in a public place, and we're seen by all the others in the gym."

"That means nothing." Sam fumed. "He could follow you home, he could purposely injure you in the gym. He could tamper with your car. You're not safe Julia."

Julia took some time to evaluate his concerns. "Sam, I have no choice but to continue down this road. I allowed one criminal to cheat justice years ago,' she sobbed. "You know my history. You know there was no way to convict the man who beat and raped me years ago."

Julia's blood ran cold, and her pulse quickened. The still vivid memory of her decades-old ordeal shook her to the core. In a flurry of vivid flashbacks, she recalled her fury at her attacker and Sam, the cop in charge of her unsolved case. Sam had been the target of her rage at the time. He had been unable to arrest the Person of Interest involved in her attack due to the lack of evidence of her assault, and therefore it became a cold case.

"Sam, I made a vow years ago to never rest if I ever witnessed injustice again. I can't betray my oath to step forward and do the right thing. I was unfortunate enough to be a victim, not only of a crime but of a system that was unable to prosecute a guilty man. I can't allow that to happen again."

Shaking his head, Sam wrung his hands in conflict. He understood Julia's reasoning but feared for her safety. He tried again to dissuade her. "Julia, you're smarter than he is, but you're no match for him physically. He's a fitness trainer! For God's sake, get real." He paused for a few minutes to let that sink in. "Goddamn it, Julia. I respect your devotion to justice, but you can't handle this alone. We need to come up with a better plan."

CHAPTER 30
JASON'S FANTASIES

It was one of those down days when Jason was enjoying a pretty relaxed schedule. He went out for an early run, then returned home, showered, and had free time to take stock of his life, his livelihood, and his accomplishments. He concluded that all was going well. Sure, there were some complications with difficult clients but for the most part, he knew how to deal with them. And the ones he couldn't deal with? Well, he had ways to take care of them. Permanently.

He understood life was hard and unfair, but he managed to cope. Getting even was what got him through rough times. There never was a reason to negotiate, to settle, or to compromise. Those were coping skills only employed by the weak. He judged himself to be stronger than any of his adversaries. And smarter too.

Jason knew the cops were keeping an eye on him and his actions but, he reasoned, they'd never figure out his game, never find evidence of his deeds, and never find his gun. The cops had already searched his living quarters and had come up with zero. Dummies like them surely would move on, eventually move away from him as a suspect and find some other poor schnook. Jason believed being considered a person of interest gave him an advantage. Aware the detectives were investigating his behaviors encouraged him to take precautions, cover his tracks, and make sure he appeared harmless. He just had to remember to control his anger and keep his rage in check.

In spite of his feelings of superiority, Jason reasoned he should have a Plan B just in case the cops got a little too nosy. He was sure he could outsmart them but didn't want to be bothered with legal hassles, more questioning, and further searches. He thought about relocating, moving on, dropping out. He could find work as a personal trainer anywhere and could easily give up his apartment. A new location might be fun and if he moved out of state, he believed the cops would lose track of him.

Jason also had second thoughts about where he had hidden his gun. In hindsight, he reasoned that telling Barbara about hiding things at one's place of employment wasn't the smartest thing he had ever said. Sure, he trusted this new client of his, nevertheless, it may have been a mistake to reveal too much information about a hiding place. She might not share that information with anyone, but he was sorry he had discussed that idea with her. Ultimately Jason decided to remove the gun from its hiding place behind the air-conditioning vent in the ceiling of the gym's men's room.

Jason gave some thought to finding a new location in which to stash his weapon. His gun was important. It had an identity of its own; it was his status symbol. It was his means of defense. It had become his friend and it removed the undesirables from his life. It eliminated the drags on society and ended the burden of carrying losers who couldn't contribute anything. Nodding his head in approval, Jason resolved to retrieve his gun tomorrow and ensconce it in a more suitable and secret location.

He lounged in his easy chair listening to the music that blasted from his stereo and allowed his mind to wander. His newest client, Barbara something-or-other, (he could never remember names), was a mystery to him. She paid for her training lessons in cash, never by check, and her payments were never in arrears. It seemed money was not a problem for her, yet she complained her ex-husband was cheap and always wanted something from her that she couldn't provide. Although her clothes looked pricey, she told him she had to hang on to a small, inexpensive cabin in the mountains since it was all that she had from her divorce settlement. Jason never asked her where she worked or what she did. The truth was, he didn't care just as long as he got paid.

Jason lazily thought about the recent invitation he had extended to Barbara. After generously inviting her to join him for a picnic in the park, his offer of friendship had been rebuffed. The stuck-up bitch gave some weak excused about why she couldn't join him. Perhaps he was wrong in assuming she was trustworthy? Perhaps he needed to be more cautious in their exchanges and more close-mouthed with the information he revealed. Perhaps he'd give her one more opportunity to accept his offer to spend more time together?

Jason played with the idea of offering her another olive branch of friendship and non-workout time together. It would be a test of her trustworthiness and he could better evaluate her dependability and loyalty.

After making a bite of lunch, Jason returned to the comfort of his living room chair, sandwich in hand. He chewed slowly, his thoughts returning to Barbara. She was pretty, physically strong, but weak when it came to dealing with her demanding ex-husband. "She needs to be taught how to be tough," he thought. "A strong man could teach her the ropes, show her how to take the verbal and physical blows, and how to dish out shit in return. She also needs to get laid," he concluded.

Jason thought that Barbara didn't know what was good for her. He assumed she was too frightened to stand up to her former spouse and too insecure to make demands of her own. Slowly Jason began to convince himself that he needed to be the catalyst in Barbara's life.

He would be the strong man who would teach her. But he would also be wary and suspicious about her intentions. His narcissism assured him that he should be the man to shape and mold her into a stronger version of herself, but she would still bend to his will and his power. She would show gratitude for his strength and guidance. She would yield to his needs and give in to his desires. She would become his creation, his servant, his possession. And she would learn to appreciate his leadership.

Jason sprang from his easy chair and reached for his phone. "Hi, Barbara. Instead of exercising in the gym next Sunday, let's do a run in the mountains. It's time you got into jogging, and I know just the right place. Have you ever been to Vasquez Rocks?" he asked.

Since Jason was the only person who could be calling on her burn phone, Julia had answered right away. Shifting into character as Barbara, she hesitated and then answered.

"Um, no, I've never been there."

"Okay then, let's meet at the gym and drive up there. Block out some extra time so we won't feel rushed."

Jason's fantasies grew even though Barbara did not confirm his invitation. Nevertheless, he knew Vasquez Rocks was a beautiful place, quiet in the early morning hours, and a romantic setting where he speculated he would fuck her.

CHAPTER 31
DISCONNECT

Immediately after disconnecting Jason's call, Julia realized she had made a mistake and spoken too quickly. "Oh, my God," she thought. "Vasquez Rocks is the place where the police found a body, shot with the same gun used in the other murders. "There's no way I can go there with him," she voiced aloud.

This was the second time Jason had suggested they visit a murder scene. Julia was beside herself with worry and fear, yet she was unable to remove herself from the center of this whirl of violence. Ultimately, she decided she must discuss these events with Sam and the police. She'd continue down the path she'd chosen but would be more accepting of police involvement and protection.

Julia checked her notes and reviewed the news clippings reporting the murder at Vasquez Rocks. The victim's remains were found days after his death. Reportedly, he was identified as Dick Stein, a young man who appeared to be in good health and physically fit. As reported, the police had no leads. The crime scene was graphically described in gory detail. According to an unnamed source, blood was found everywhere. Mr. Stein was shot once, and the police had no leads.

Closing her notebook, Julia, sure the killer was Jason Montgomery, decided to take a leap of faith. Jason usually called to confirm the time and place a day or so before each scheduled appointment. She decided she would boldly tell Jason when he called that she felt spooked going to Vasquez Rocks, a reported murder scene. She'd fain fear of the murderer returning, planning to commit more violence. Perhaps Jason might even make a slip and divulge some meaningful evidence? Perhaps he'd tell her not to worry because he knew she'd be safe?

As planned, when Jason called Julia, she explained why she didn't want to go. His simple answer was, "Okay."

Both relief and disappointment flooded over Julia simultaneously. Not sure if avoiding a trip to Vasquez Rocks was a missed opportunity to question him more closely or an act of safety,

Julia was determined not to let the topic of that location lapse. She would talk about it again and try to dig deeper when she next met with Jason.

Ending the phone conversation, Julia felt a bit better knowing the Vasquez Rocks destination was off the table. At least for the immediate future, a weight had been lifted and she felt more at ease.

For Jason, the impact of their brief phone conversation produced the opposite effect, and he was filled with high anxiety. "Shit. She's not so dumb. She knows something about Vazquez. Christ, that was months ago. Why does she remember it? How much does she know? How many questions will she ask? Does she scan the media for crime reports? Is this the only report she remembers, or will she connect this to any others?"

Jason began to sweat. He desperately tried to recall past conversations they had and struggled to remember if anything of importance had been discussed. He recalled telling her a good hiding place for things she didn't want to be discovered would be at work.

"I can't be too careful with this broad," he reasoned. "She may be trouble. And if she's looking for trouble, I can give it to her," he vowed to himself. "I've been too nice, too giving, too trusting. I'm glad I decided to move the gun. Shit, why'd I tell her the best place to hide things was at work? That was a mistake. Now I'll have to find a way to shut the bitch up." Once again, Jason's mania controlled his thinking and convinced him that he was smarter than everyone.

CHAPTER 32
THIS IS OUTRAGEOUS

"This is outrageous, and I don't like the idea at all. Leave the detective work to us. You're in over your head." Detective Roberta Phelps's voice contained no hint of sympathy as she continued to admonish Julia.

"Julia, we know you want to help but you're not a trained detective and you should not be seeing Montgomery. He's a monster and you're exposing yourself to extreme danger. We really appreciate the help you've already provided, and your astute observations gave us a more solid direction in pursuing the case, but now it's time to stop."

Julia took some time before answering. Drawing strength from a deep breath she slowly turned to both detectives, Roberta Phelps, and Steven Rich. "You can't prevent me from employing the trainer of my choice. I'm a private citizen and I have the right to decide what I want to do and with whom."

"Be reasonable, we can't assign a bodyguard to accompany you," Rich added.

"I'm not asking for protection. I'm here only to inform you that I think Montgomery has hidden the murder weapon somewhere at his gym. He gave me that idea because he trusts me and let down his guard. He volunteered a piece of advice about where to hide things; it wasn't obtained illegally or under duress. His advice was freely given."

The small meeting room fell quiet as the group of four sat silently, Phelps and Rich sat facing Julia and Sam across the table. Rich picked up the discussion, "Okay, let's look at our options. Julia, you're right, we can't prevent you from meeting and working out with Montgomery, and we can't provide any details that would support ongoing protection."

Getting up from his chair, Rich circled the small group at the table and thought out loud. "I do think we have enough to get another search warrant for the gym. He's already a Person of Interest so I believe it's not out of line to search his place of employment." Rich abruptly stopped his walk.

"Here's the problem I see. If we find nothing, and the search comes up empty, he's gonna figure out you are the one who gave us the lead to look for the gun at the gym. Then you become his next victim."

Hiding her concern Julia protested. "Not necessarily. It's reasonable to search the place of employment of a Person of Interest. It should have been done already and he won't connect a new search with me because he trusts me."

Sam had been listening to the back and forth with careful attention. "Look, there's no getting around the fact that Julia is in danger. He could harm her when they're together, or he could follow her after she leaves the gym. I know you can't spare the manpower to protect her, but I can provide some of that security. I've been down that road more than once and I know what needs to be done."

Roberta drummed her fingers on the table. "You both are private citizens; we can't tell you what to do in your free time. As long as what you do is legal, our hands are tied."

"Nevertheless, be reasonable," Roberta insisted. "Julia, you absolutely must not go to Vasquez Rocks hiking with him. He's far too unpredictable and Sam can't provide any protection there."

"I told you, I already let Montgomery know I didn't want to go there."

"Good. But whatever you plan to do, won't be an official police operation and you'll basically be on your own. But I want you to know, I can't condone your actions."

Both Julia and Sam shook their heads in agreement.

Roberta continued, "The only official next step would be obtaining a search warrant and then conducting a search for the gun. And obtaining the warrant may take a while. My advice to you both is to sit tight, be careful, and do nothing until you hear from us. We'll let you know when we have the warrant. This meeting is over—for now." Phelps and Rich got up and left the room.

CHAPTER 33
SUSPICION CONFIRMED

Jason felt uneasy about the brief encounter with the stranger at the shooting range. The man asked too many questions and was a bit too friendly. Jason's life was getting complicated now that the police were an ever-present threat, and Jason had to be careful. Something about the exchange at the shooting range bothered him and he wasn't quite sure what had gotten under his skin.

There were periods of time when Jason ruminated over conversations and small happenstances, and this was one of those unexpected circumstances that produced apprehension and anxiety. During periods of stress Jason's moods changed quickly and he was capable of feeling either superior and invincible or vulnerable. His mood swings could be extreme. He vacillated between believing he could outsmart others and handle any situation, or feeling powerless, which made him morose.

Feeling at risk, Jason recalled his early disappointment in life. The accident that shattered his career dreams of becoming an athlete of worldwide recognition, left a bitter taste in his mouth. That acrid memory, coupled with the last several weeks of police scrutiny, left Jason spent and angry. He questioned why he had been victimized by cruel and unjust events. He deserved more, but fate dealt him an unfair hand and he needed to summon the strength to overcome the injustices he had suffered.

His thoughts turned to his sister, Alice. Jason allowed his mind to wander back to his younger days and he clearly remembered Alice's acts of kindness and encouragement. During the many difficult months of recovering from his accident, Alice, five years older, was a beacon of help and strength. It was she who tried to brighten his days. She fixed him snacks, read to him, and catered to his needs. Alice would tell him jokes and report on the comings and goings of friends.

Alice assisted him, steadied him when he tried to walk and ran errands for him. She was a constant companion with a sunny disposition.

Jason and Alice had drifted apart over the last few years. Now that she lived in Las Vegas, they saw each other infrequently and spoke on the phone only occasionally. They exchanged Christmas greetings, but each had followed a different path and now the closeness and softness of their earlier relationship were clouded in a veil of history.

Putting the warm feelings of his sister, Alice, into the recesses of his memory, Jason sat in his small kitchen cleaning the weapon he used at the shooting range the day before and reviewed his meeting with the other shooter.

Not much to worry about; nothing of importance had been discussed, yet Jason didn't trust the accuracy of his memory concerning their meeting. Right now, he felt uneasy about their brief time together at the range. No, Jason thought, he just couldn't let it go. Why did this stranger ask so many questions?

With a heavy sigh, Jason decided he had to return to Gill's Guns and Ammo and ask Gill about the man who was using Bay Number 4 the day he was there. Packing his weapon away, Jason decided he'd return the gun to its new hiding spot, and then continue on to the gun store.

Jason arrived at Gill's slightly after 2:00 p.m. and was pleased to see the shop wasn't busy. Gill, behind one of the display cases, was sitting on a stool reading the newspaper.

"Hi, Gill, how ya' doing?" Jason broadly announced his arrival with this greeting. Looking up Gill, was surprised to see Jason again so soon. Recognizing Jason was a regular, and a good customer, it was nonetheless unusual for him to return after using the shooting range so recently. Gill returned the greeting with a high five.

"What can I do for you, man?"

No stranger to spinning lies Jason had concocted what he thought was a plausible explanation for this visit.

"I met this new guy here yesterday and we decided to target shoot together again. We exchanged contact information, and I wrote his name and number on a piece of paper so we could plan a get-together. Now I can't find the paper! I know I shoulda put his info on my phone but didn't have it with me at the time. Can you help me?"

"Just a minute, let me think. Oh, you mean the retired cop?"

Hearing these words, Jason, near panic, swallowed hard but showed no reaction. "A cop, a cop, shit!" he thought. "I knew the guy was trouble. This is not good." Jason smiled at Gill and nodded.

"Yeah, he's the one. Can you give me his name and number?"

Going to the file cabinet Gill retrieved the forms that listed Sam's name, address, and phone number. "Here we are. Sam Malloy and here's his phone number." Gill placed the form and the copy of Sam's driver's license on the glass-topped counter.

In what appeared to be a causal manner Jason copied the information and continued the conversation.

"Thanks, Gill. I'll take the number. Don't think I need the address, just the number will do," he lied. Jason, not wanting to arouse any suspicion, hoped only showing interest in the phone number might conceal his real intent. "I may give him a call and see if he's still interested in getting together."

Jason left the shop and knew what he had to do. The minute Jason heard that Sam was a retired cop, he realized he had to kill the SOB.

CHAPTER 34
PARALLEL STRATEGIES

As he slowly drove home from Gill's Guns and Ammo, Jason mapped out a strategy outlining what he had to do. There was no question in his mind that he had to kill Malloy. The last thing Jason wanted was some retired cop nosing around. The way Jason figured; he had no choice but to off Malloy as soon as possible. Yet, as obvious as that decision was, it was disturbing and could be dangerous, not to mention that this hit would be a total departure from his usual pattern.

Jason defined his kills as necessary because his usual victims, his fitness clients, weren't worthy of living. For one reason or another, Jason believed he was ridding society of undesirables. He reasoned it was just and appropriate to eliminate present and former clients who were deadwood drags and would never amount to anything. Malloy didn't fit into that category, but Jason believed *he had to do what he had to do.*

He turned the corner, driving ever closer to his apartment, and continued brainstorming what needed to be done. "Malloy's not a fitness client, but there's still a chance the cops could connect him to me," he mumbled aloud. "He's not a member of my gym and that puts Malloy outside the loop of the other targets. If I'm not careful, some smart-ass cop might link Malloy to me," he thought. "It's a crap-shoot. If I make the hit during the night, that will break the pattern of the mid-morning hits, so the cops might not see a connection to their so-called Mid-Morning Murders." For some unknown reason, this made him laugh.

Heaving a sigh, Jason concluded he had to make this hit look like a home invasion that led to violence. This realization put him outside his comfort zone. He fully understood he had to be careful. He'd design a tactic and develop a game plan that would accomplish his deadly goal and leave no clues or hints that would lead the cops to suspect him.

Thinking back over the last few months of police scrutiny and questioning, Jason felt the ordeal had gone on for too long, but he also was sure the police would continue to hit a brick wall in their investigation.

Nearing his street, Jason glanced at the dashboard clock. "Wow, it's three-thirty already. I must have been at Gill's for more than an hour," he realized. Now a bit closer to finding the right solution to the Malloy conundrum, Jason began to feel more secure about his future.

"I'll get rid of Malloy, mess up his house, make it look like a robbery, and get that retired cop out of the picture." Once again, he chuckled at the thought of the moniker given to his activities. "Mid-Morning Murders, eh? Well, this next one won't fit the expected MO."

A scant number of miles away, another strategic planning session was in progress. Julia, Sam, and Detectives Rich and Phelps were again assembled around the table in the police station's conference room. And their game plan had begun to parallel Jason's in reasoning and structure!

"We've got to find a solution to end this Mid-Morning Murder conundrum," Julia said.

"You're right. We have to come up with new tactics and develop a new game plan to accomplish our primary goal: arrest and conviction of this dirtbag," Phelps announced.

"Until then, we can't feel secure about the future."

"Montgomery's a slippery character, so we have to be careful. This investigation has gone on far too long and we've hit a brick wall too many times. I had hoped we'd find Montgomery's gun when we searched the gym, but we came up empty. There was nothing there."

Julia remained silent and bit her lip. It was at her insistence that the police had checked the gym for Montgomery's gun. She felt now that this had been a mistake.

The conversation between the four continued. Phelps leaned in, moving closer to Julia. "Look, this is a tough case, and we have real departures from our usual patterns of operation here." She paused for effect. "I don't have to remind you," she nodded indicating Sam and Julia, "I'm out of my comfort zone with both of you running amok doing your own thing."

Phelps continued, "Julia, I'm totally against your workout activities with the suspect. If you and Sam don't stop interfering in this case, we'll put you in protective custody for your own good. You and Sam are fucking up our investigation. Don't meddle here. It's unacceptable. I don't approve of your meetings with Montgomery, and although I can't stop you, I want you to understand it's not a good thing."

Detective Rich continued the admonishment and directed his words to Sam. "I know you want to map out a strategy to close the case, Sam, but following Montgomery and trying to foster a relationship with him, although not illegal, is dangerous. Stay out of it."

Although the cops' words were stern, Julia and Sam dismissed their warnings and disapproval. Determined to continue their efforts to prove Jason guilty, they minimized the cops' threats to place them in protective custody.

There was no question they would continue their activities. Julia and Sam nodded in agreement but said nothing.

Glancing at the wall clock, Julia noted, "Wow, it's almost three-thirty. We've been at this for more than an hour and haven't resolved much. I assume you two will continue following leads and hunches until there's a real breakthrough."

Detective Phelps smiled encouragingly at Julia attempting to soften her earlier warnings to stay out of trouble and bow out of direct contact with Montgomery. "Yes, of course," Phelps said. "Until then let's keep each other informed of any progress made."

Julia simply replied, "Sam and I will try to be more restrained and not interfere in your work but if we see or hear anything pertinent, we'll let you know. Let's keep our lines of communication and coordination intact."

Each participant left the meeting feeling little had been accomplished. Montgomery was an adversary who was both methodical and experienced. He showed no hint of ending his murderous rampage and both Julia and Sam realized they could be next on his hit list. But they also believed *they had to do what they had to do.*

CHAPTER 35
QUITTING IS NOT AN OPTION

"What's wrong Julia? You're not yourself, lately," Matt queried. I've been worried about you the last couple of weeks."

"I'm just tired, that's all," she replied with a hint of sadness. Julia was stretched out on the sofa facing Matt who was seated on the easy chair in their den. Matt leaned forward, rubbed his hands together, and shook his head.

"You're talking to me. I know you better than that. I don't buy it. Tell me what's going on," he gently said.

Suddenly Julia began to cry softly. Finding it difficult to speak she brushed away the tears and reached for her husband's hand. "I love you Matt and I don't want you to worry about me. It's just that I feel I have too many balls in the air right now, and it's getting hard to balance them all."

Nodding his head in agreement, Matt moved to the sofa. "Let's talk about it. How can I help?"

"Between the job, don't get me wrong, I love the work and the house and kids, and…and," her voice trailed off. Julia paused for a few minutes and then continued.

"Well, you know I've been going to the gym and working out with Jason. You know the history here; you know he's the cop's person of interest. And he's kinda scary."

"Yes, and I told you I'm not happy about it. I also told you I'd rearrange my gym time and place to coincide with yours. We could meet at his gym. He'd never know our connection to each other. Do you want me to do that?"

"No. I don't feel I'm in danger when we're at the gym. It's safe there. It's just a long drive, exhausting, and very time-consuming." Julia blew her nose and again wiped her eyes. "And I just hate him."

"Then stop this. You've already done more than enough to help the police and Sam is very capable of assisting them if they need his help. I think both of you should butt out. Let the professionals do their job."

"You sound just like Phelps and Rich. That's what they said when we met with them yesterday. They even threatened to put us in protective custody if we don't back off."

"Well, what are you waiting for?"

"Matt, you know I can't. First of all, I've come too far to back off. Secondly, I'm committed to obtaining justice and punishment where indicated. It's now almost part of my DNA. I'm compelled to see this through because of my past experience with justice being denied. If I quit now, I couldn't face myself in the mirror."

"For goodness sake, Julia! You're not a quitter. Don't ever think that. You're braver and stronger than anyone I know. Ending your involvement isn't a sign of weakness or quitting. It's a show of strength and independence to protect yourself."

It was easy to see and understand Julia's struggle. As a lawyer, Julia was dedicated to upholding the law. As a private citizen, wife, and mother, she was devoted to fairness and impartiality. As the survivor of a long-ago unsolved criminal attack, she yearned to find closure for other victims. Her intense longing for justice in her own case was equaled by her longing to bring justice and closure to others. There was no way she could sleep nights if Jason was never punished.

"I promise you, Matt, I'll take whatever precautions are needed. I won't work out with him anyplace other than the gym. But I can't stop. At least not until the police find his gun. Proving his gun is the weapon used in all the crimes is the key. Once they conclusively connect his firearm to the murders, I'll back off."

CHAPTER 36
DANGER ARRIVES

"Let's get some snacks out Maisie. You can't have a poker game without stuff to munch on." Sam puttered around in his kitchen readying everything for his weekly poker game. "It's a little after seven and the guys will be here soon."

"Hmmm. Nuts, chips, dip, and I think maybe some cheese and crackers will do it," he informed Maisie as he carried the trays to the dining room table. "The beer is already in the fridge, so I think we're all set." Maisie wagged her tail indicating agreement. "And how about a biscuit for you, good girl?" Sam said as he returned to the kitchen. Following Sam's every move, the dog excitedly waited for her treat.

Feeling relaxed and happily anticipating the arrival of his friends, Sam continued taking to Masie.

"I have just enough time to put on a clean shirt and freshen up before the hungry hordes get here," he joked.

The light sound of a footstep approaching the front porch alerted Sam to an early arriving guest. "Come on in, the door's open, you early bird." Sam, still in the kitchen, called out. "I'll be right there."

Jason confidently entered the house, took a small breath, and looked around. His gun, already drawn, was firmly held in his hand. He said nothing, remaining coldly silent, and waited for Sam to enter the room.

"Hi, how about – hey, what are you doing here?" Sam stammered in confusion. Immediately Sam recognized Jason and knew he was in grave danger.

"I thought we were going to have a shooting date at Gill's range, not at my house," Sam said. He tried to sound funny and unconcerned.

"We're not going to have any target shooting date, you fucker. Who do you think you are? You can't follow me around and stick your nose in my business." Jason's voice started to rise, and his anger was palpable.

"Now hold on. I've not been following you. We just met at Gill's, and I thought we could be pals." Sam explained.

"Stop lying, you're working with the cops," Jason yelled.

"No way, that's ridiculous. Why would I do something like that?" Sam hoped engaging Jason in conversation might diminish Jason's fury and also provide time for Sam to find a way to defend himself. His years on the police force equipped him to think clearly under duress and remain calm.

As Sam struggled to defuse Jason's rage, the killer's uncontrollable hatred intensified. Jason's shouting increased. The escalating noise of his argument drew Maisie to Sam's side. Jason raised his gun and took careful aim at Sam's chest. He took a step forward, facing Sam, and pulled the trigger.

Seconds before the bullet was discharged, Maisie leaped across the short distance between the two men, attacking Jason and deflecting his aim as the bullet exited the gun's barrel. She vaulted high in the air, growling, and repeatedly bit Jason's hand and wrist. Maisie continued her assault while he struggled to get away. Finally, able to release himself from the dog's grip, the shock and pain of the attack were so acute that Jason dropped his gun, clutching his injured right hand.

As Sam fell to the floor, Jason ran from the room.

CHAPTER 37
I FEEL SO MUCH BETTER

Unaware of the recent violence that occurred at Sam's cottage, Julia and Matt spent a quiet evening at home. For the moment at least both felt secure and content. The tumultuous activity and dangerous encounters of the last few months left them spent but also happy to be able to enjoy some quiet time together.

They listened to some soft music, talked about the kids, and tried to behave as if they had not a care in the world. The whirlwind of police work swirling around them was tossed aside as best as possible. Together they had vowed to remove all unpleasant thoughts and fears. Tonight would be a special night with no intrusive thoughts or anxiety.

"I feel so much better," Julia said. She was curled in Matt's arms. "I finally feel a weight has been lifted from my shoulders and I can breathe again." She smiled and snuggled closer to her husband. Her mood had been lifted, not just improved by their recent lovemaking, but also by the knowledge that she and Matt could talk honestly and get through difficult situations together.

Expressing her fear and apprehension to him alleviated some of her anxiety and his reassurance that he would always protect and defend her lessened her tension. She was grateful that their recent conversation had cleared the air and that Matt understood her need to continue her involvement with the police. They kept no secrets from each other and realized truthfulness and trust were as intimately linked as they were.

Matt's understanding, although coupled with his concern, filled her with gratitude and love. His support was something she had always valued. He had been her rock in the past, and now, once again, he showed his strength by backing up her decision to take risks she believed necessary. He had made it clear he wasn't happy about her taking chances, but he recognized her passion and perceived obligation to do so.

This wasn't easy for Matt. At times he struggled, fearful she might expose herself to too many risks, but he also knew if he intervened, she'd lose confidence and self-respect.

"With you at my side, and Sam's experience, I'll survive," she mused, snuggling closer to Matt. "I've learned a lot from Sam, and he knows what steps to take so Detectives Rich and Phelps don't arrest us for obstructing their investigation," she joked half-heartedly.

"Yeah, the two of you could wind up behind bars before Jason Montgomery!" Matt cautioned, wrapping his arms around her. "Just remember you're a lawyer and you can't afford to jeopardize your reputation or license to practice."

"Sam's been terrific and I'm glad he reached out to me; that we have reconnected after so many years. Who would have ever believed we'd forge a friendship after such a rocky relationship in the past?"

"Once this Mid-Morning mystery is solved and Montgomery is in custody, I'm sure we'll enjoy a more traditional friendship with Sam, one not based on clues, missing guns, or body counts." Matt toyed with a curl on Julia's shoulder while contemplating a less stressful future.

"And, you know what else?" He continued. "When this ordeal is finally over, let's take a vacation with the kids." Matt described a trip he and Julia might take with Hillary and Bobbie. He painted a fanciful escapade to some beautiful and exotic location where they could relax and forget the trauma of the last few months.

"Oh, that would be wonderful," Julia murmured half asleep. "The kids would love it and so would I. I want to feel sand beneath my feet and a warm breeze caressing my skin. Perhaps we could go to some island and escape reality even for a short while." Matt kissed her lightly and stroked her hair.

"I love you," he whispered. "And when this is all finished, we'll put the bad memories away and never think about them again. Life will return to normal," He promised.

"I hope so," Julia whispered as she fell asleep.

CHAPTER 38
ON THE RUN

"Shit, I shoulda shot the dog, too." Jason hastily made his way to his parked car, hidden at the far end of the lane where Sam's cottage was located. "That animal's more like a rabid wolf than a dog," he swore as he grasped his bleeding hand.

"At least," he reasoned, "no one saw me. But that damn dog made enough noise to cause problems." Once inside his car, Jason thought about his next moves, outlining the steps he needed to take.

"Shit, shit, shit," he yelled and repeatedly pounded the steering wheel with his uninjured fist. I dropped my fucking gun there because of that fucking dog. "I have to go back and get it."

In a frenzy of uncertainty, Jason turned his car around and headed back down the lane toward the cottage. Approaching Sam's cottage Jason saw the headlights of another vehicle turn and enter Sam's driveway.

"Fuck! What? Is he getting company now?" Jason screamed. "Well, they're gonna find a dead host," he said sarcastically. Sure that the dog, now barking, frantically, had alerted neighbors, Jason's hope of retrieving his gun was ruined. "Fuck, fuck, fuck," he shouted again and again.

Slowly, he began to realize he was now a fugitive. There was no other option for him but to run. Mentally he formulated a list of places where he could hide, places where he would not be found, places where he could live undetected.

Jason nervously bit his lip. He realized leaving the gun behind was a major problem. But it was too dangerous to return to Sam's cottage and he was fully aware that he had to put distance between himself and the current crime scene.

In his frenzy, he briefly thought about barging into the cottage, retrieving the weapon, and overpowering the new arrival. He pictured himself bullying and threatening whoever had just arrived, grabbing the gun, and then retreating. But he recognized that would be a mistake. Perhaps there was more than one visitor at Sam's cottage, and then, there was the damn dog! Putting the car in drive, Jason headed to his apartment. He would sort out his next steps, pack some necessary items, grab some money, establish an alibi, and make a clean getaway.

He drove quickly, but his thoughts of escape were tangled and interrupted by fear of apprehension. But within minutes his narcissism took over, permitting him to rationalize his conduct and deeds. He perceived his superior intelligence would get him through this unexpected misstep and he'd find a way out of this dilemma. He cursed, wondering why fate always dealt him a lousy hand. But, always believing his actions were justified, Jason was able to defend his behavior.

Halfway home, he had already developed a plan. He'd fire off some quick texts to each of his clients scheduled for the next few weeks, explaining that he was called out of town on a family emergency and then he'd drive to Las Vegas.

His loving, supportive sister, Alice, would provide the alibi he needed. Besides, no one would ever connect him to Alice.

CHAPTER 39
A VERY CLOSE CALL

Julia bolted upright in bed. The blaring ring of the phone rippled through her body and immediately put her into a state of alarm. Why would someone be calling at two in the morning?

"Yes, yes, I got it," Julia grunted in a husky sleep dazed voice. "How does it look? Yes, I'll be there as soon as possible."

Matt turned to her inquisitively. "What's going on?"

"Get dressed. Sam's been shot. He's at the hospital. It doesn't look good," Julia hastily explained. She spoke in barely audible, short sentences, hardly catching her breath between words.

"I'll call Mrs. Jackson and tell her it's an emergency and we need her to get here as soon as possible to babysit. She's only two minutes away." Matt reached for his cell phone on the bedside table.

Immediately after Mrs. Jackson's arrival, Julia and Matt raced to the car scarcely speaking, each afraid to speculate about what had happened and what the outcome might be. The short ride to the hospital seemed an interminable destination in spite of the fact that they were speeding.

As Matt negotiated the roadway, Julia struggled to control her fears while concentrating on what needed to be done. The dreadful phone call informing her that Sam had been shot came from Roberta Phelps, so the detectives were already aware. With an overwhelming feeling of sorrow, Julia realized she didn't know if Sam had any close family or distant relatives to be called.

Mentally Julia developed a list of questions to ask upon arriving at the hospital. The first, indeed, the most important, was Sam's condition and his chance of survival.

They rode the elevator to the Intensive Care Unit as directed. They exchanged not a word, not a glance. They silently shared worry and fear but little else. Her throat dry, her hands sweaty, and her heartbreaking, Julia stepped out of the elevator and was met by Detective Phelps.

"How is he?" she asked.

"Hard to say. It's touch and go. He's out of surgery and the docs say he won't be out of the woods for a while yet," Roberta reported. Looking tired and worried Roberta said nothing more.

They sat in the waiting room in a small knot where others were also anxiously waiting for news of their loved ones. At the far end of the room, a lone sleeping man waited to hear about his elderly wife. In a corner of the room, a couple prayed for the recovery of a family member in a car accident.

Footsteps on the tile floors echoed the movements of those who ventured off seeking coffee. In the wee hours of the morning the waiting area, bleak and quiet, was desolate and grim.

Huddled together Roberta filled Julia and Matt in on what she had learned.

"Sam's very lucky," she began. "It seems he was shot immediately before friends arrived for their weekly poker game." She paused and took a sip of coffee, warming her hands on the cup she held before continuing.

"If they had been late, Sam would be a goner for sure. Their timely arrival and quick thinking saved his life. One of the men is a doctor, the other a pharmacist, and together they knew what to do. They immediately called for help."

Hearing this, Julia closed her eyes and said a silent thank you for their quick arrival and knowledge.

Roberta continued. "We'll all say a prayer and cross our fingers that he makes it, but for sure, these friends of Sam's at least gave him a fighting chance."

Again, Roberta turned her attention to her coffee cup, one of the few things that helped keep her awake at this early hour.

"We have more good news," she continued. "Whoever was in that house and shot Sam wasn't very tidy. He dropped his gun. Right now, it's being examined, and the ballistics report should tell us if it's a match for the other murders. This is a really important find."

"Oh, my God, this is big," Julia almost shouted.

"Wait, there's more good news." Roberta smiled as she said this. "We found blood droplets, not likely Sam's. They aren't near where he fell. We think Maisie, the dog, attacked the intruder. If so, when the tests are complete, we may have the perp's blood evidence."

All this newly collected evidence encouraged them to have hope for more positive news. As the sun rose and daylight dawned, they were joined by some of Sam's poker-playing friends, Detective Rich, and a few cops who knew Sam and had learned of the shooting. They sat together, all hoping for the best.

CHAPTER 40
PROGNOSIS

Sam's medical prognosis remained uncertain. Leaving him in the capable hands of the Intensive Care Unit staff, Matt and Julia returned home, and the detectives returned to the precinct to wait for the results of the blood tests and ballistic reports.

Exhausted, but too stressed out to sleep, Julia made a pot of coffee and she and Matt sat down and discussed the events of the night. "What happens next?" Matt asked his wife.

"I don't know. Right now, I'm just hoping Sam recovers, and that he will be able to tell us what happened and who shot him."

"Well, isn't it obvious that it was that shithead, Jason?"

Julia nodded her head, yes. "But just because we're certain he was the shooter doesn't prove anything. The blood droplets and ballistic reports, along with an I.D. from Sam, would make the case stick."

"Why don't the cops go to Jason's apartment and pick him up and question him right now?" Matt queried.

"I guess they're waiting for the reports to confirm what they suspect but can't yet prove."

Matt reflected on his wife's analysis of the situation. "Julia, this is dangerous. You need to protect yourself. You could be a target just like Sam. You used to be a good shot when we went target shooting in the past. I think you should start carrying a gun. I realize it's been a while, so I think you should take our gun out to the range and start practicing again."

Julia looked at her husband with concern. "Do you really think it necessary? I haven't shot a gun in quite a while."

"Yes, it would make me feel more secure knowing you're armed, and your carrying permit and license are still valid."

Julia and Matt continued the discussion and eventually, Julia reluctantly agreed to carry the weapon. She promised to practice and review all the safety protocols and renew her membership at the range.

The two of them, too tired to continue speculations sat in silence sipping their coffee. It was late-morning and both Matt and Julia were grateful that Mrs. Jackson had spent the night and helped the twins get off to school. She was a gold mine of dependability and competence, and they were lucky they could call upon her for last minute childcare. The house was quiet now with the kids away, and there was little either of them could do to assist the detectives with their investigation.

Seeking some soothing sound to help her relax, Julia inserted a CD into the player and programed some soft music. As the melodic sounds filled the air, Julia checked all the phones for any messages that might have arrived earlier.

She was shocked to read the following text from Jason Montgomery: *"Due to a family emergency, I am canceling our scheduled workout appointments. I will be out of town for the next several weeks."*

"Oh my God!" Julia murmured. "The bastard's on the run."

"Wait, what?" Matt looked up from his coffee cup with renewed interest and concern.

Julia shared the message contained in the text. She paused and thought about its meaning. She repeated the phrases family emergency and out of town several times. Shaking her head from side to side, Julia whispered "No, no way."

Matt moved closer and put his arm around her. "What are you thinking? What's going on in your head?"

"He has no family other than his sister, Alice, in Las Vegas. That's where he's going. I have to call Roberta Phelps."

CHAPTER 41
TIGHTENING THE NOOSE

"Thanks for getting here so quickly," Roberta said as she ushered Julia into the   meeting. A small group of detectives was huddled in the room where they were studying the just released results of the lab and ballistics tests, as well as the examination of the gun left behind in Sam's cottage.

"There's no question about it now. Montgomery's the Mid-Morning guy. The bullet that shot Sam is a match and came from the same gun used in the Jeffreys, Preston, and Stein murders."

Julia sank into her chair and heaved a great sigh of relief. " What about the blood droplets?" she asked.

"We're still waiting on that. We went to the dirtbag's apartment with a warrant, planning to collect some DNA and to arrest him, but he's gone." Roberta paused, shook her head, and studied the notes, reports, and diagrams pinned to the corkboard on the wall. "We've got an all-points bulletin out and some roadblocks up thanks to your tip that he may be headed to his sister in Las Vegas. Do you have anything more specific on that lead?"

"I've been desperately trying to remember what Jason told me about his sister, Alice. It was quite a while ago, and I'm sure he's forgotten that he told me he had a sister, but the most I can recall is that she works at one of the bigger Las Vegas casinos. I'm not sure which one or what she does there but I'm pretty sure she works at one of them."

"Okay, we've contacted the Las Vegas Police Department and we will try to coordinate with them to track down this sister, Alice. Do you know her last name?" Roberta asked.

"No," was Julia's first response but after pausing for a few seconds she added, "If Alice works at a gambling establishment, and is on the casino floor, she must have been required to get a Sheriff's Card from the Nevada Gaming Control Board."

"Right," Roberta cheered. "Good thought. We'll get on that and check the Nevada licensing records and see if an Alice Montgomery somebody-or-other is licensed. That should give us an address."

Roberta continued, "Fortunately, established laws allow both California and Nevada reciprocity rights, and detectives from either state may pursue and arrest felons who flee from one jurisdiction to the other. It is, however, customary for police departments to inform each other of any plans to cross state lines. I'm sure that LVPD will be willing to work with us."

Detective Steven Rich chimed in. "That's right. Inter-jurisdictional guidelines allow us to assist officers from other jurisdictions and vice versa. Law officers from different locations frequently work together to coordinate logistics and supply additional personnel as needed, and we could use the extra help on this case." Continuing his explanation, Rich added, "Many states have agreements to work cooperatively."

Roberta turned to Steven, who had been actively involved in studying the results of the various forensic tests and asked him to follow up on contacting the Las Vegas Police Department and the Nevada Gaming Control Board.

"Sure thing, Roberta. I'm already on the line with the LVPD and we're working on it."

Feeling like they were finally making progress, the stress and tension in the room dissipated somewhat. Instead of frenzy, those in the room settled down to what could best be described as hyperactivity. They wanted this asshole. They wanted him bad. And they would leave no stone unturned to find and convict this brazen killer.

The buzz in the room was interrupted by the ringing of Roberta's phone. "Yes, yes, oh that's good," was all she said before she disconnected the call. "Sam's awake," she smiled.

CHAPTER 42
FAMILY REUNION

It was near morning, and he had driven through the night. The good thing about driving to Las Vegas before dawn is there's little traffic and you can make time. As he flew over the speed limit, Jason concocted a story hoping to enlist sympathy and cooperation from his sister, Alice. Merely telling her he missed her and wanted to visit wouldn't do the trick and he knew he'd have to be more creative. He needed a cover story with urgency and danger that would activate Alice's ability to swallow tall tales and keep secrets, but most importantly, protect him. He believed she could be trusted but at the very least, Jason had to make his lie sound reasonable.

He found her apartment easily, not far from The Strip, where he assumed, she was employed. Confident she'd be home at this early hour he sat in his car rehearsing his false narrative. Accustomed to lying, Jason was able to invent fanciful fibs that skirted the truth and were vague enough to be believed. Assured that he was well prepared, Jason rang his sister's doorbell.

Still dressed in her nightgown and bathrobe, Alice looked through the door's peephole and was stunned to see her brother standing there smiling. "Good Lord! What brings you to Las Vegas, stranger?" she asked, sounding both surprised and pleased. "Where the hell have you been, and what have you been up to? It's been an age."

She threw the door wide open, grabbed her brother by the shoulders, and dragged him in with one huge bear hug. "Ya coulda called and I'd a had breakfast ready."

Somewhat surprised by this very warm welcome, Jason followed her into the kitchen as she put up coffee and searched the refrigerator for some breakfast fixings. "Sit down and catch me up while I make us something to eat," Alice instructed.

Jason started with what he thought to be the standard greetings and "long lost" relative B.S. He rattled off the usual list of comments on one's life: I've been fine, I've been busy, had a few dates, missed the family, needed a change of scenery, and so on. He rambled on and finally got to the point of his visit. Lowering his voice, he became more serious. "Sis, I need a favor from you. Could you please…"

Interrupting him mid-sentence, Alice shook her head in protest. "Jason, not money again. I just bought new tires for my old car, and I'm tapped out. I can't see my way to…"

"No, no. I don't want any money but I'm in a jam. I paid off some loan sharks and I'm clear with the debt, but the two SOBs hassled me before the payoff. Before I could give them the envelope with the cash in it my gun accidentally went off and I think I clipped one of them. The second guy grabbed his buddy and the money, and they both took off."

"Oh my God, Jason. Why do you deal with these people? You shot someone? Is he okay? Christ, I didn't even know you owned a gun! Did the police come?"

"No. I told you, the second guy helped the other one limp away. There's no way he'd go to the police. And I got rid of my gun. I'm unarmed now. I threw it in a lake so there'd be no way the police could find or trace it."

Jason was aware Alice was also a gun owner and he hoped she'd believe his lie about throwing his gun away. "Christ," he thought. "She's a by-the-book bore", and she'll know owners don't throw their weapons away. But he had to appear vulnerable and defenseless.

"Jason, I don't understand your behavior. You always seem to have one problem or another that needs fixing. I can't keep helping you out. Leave me out of it. There's nothing I can do to help you."

"Yes, there is a way you can help." Jason paused as if in thought although he already knew exactly what his request would be. He had carefully developed his plan but wanted his sister to think he was struggling to find a way she could help.

"I doubt there will be any problems. There's no way those thugs will figure out where I am. But on the outside chance, they find me, I'd like to borrow your gun, just for self-defense. I really doubt that will happen, but you know, just in case. They could be looking to get even."

"Are you nuts? No."

"Look, this is Vegas, an open carry state. Everyone here has a gun and you told me a while ago you bought one for when you come home late after a graveyard shift at the casino."

"Stop this. I've had enough. I can't keep fixing things for you. Are the police looking for the person who shot this guy?"

"I dunno. I doubt it. But, if the police or those SOBs who hassled me come looking, I want you to tell them, you haven't seen me, and you don't know where I am. I'll stay here only a day or two, until things quiet down and then move on."

"Say you're not here and I haven't seen you? What if the cops come? You want me to lie to the cops? I can't jeopardize my gaming license by lying to the police. My job is my bread and butter, and I can't risk losing it. If they ever found out I lied to the police, I'd be fired for sure."

"Don't make this a bigger deal than it is. Chances are no one knows where I am, and no one will show up. The possibility of the cops coming here is zero to none. Listen to me. You owe me this favor and I'll clear out of here as soon as I've rested. I need some money, your gun, some supplies, and then I'm outa here."

"I owe you nothing. I've always been there for you and now you want me to lie and cover for you. You can take my gun if you must, but then go."

Alice watched the expression on Jason's face cloud over, becoming one she had never seen before. She was surprised and frightened by his insistence and his threatening tone. Jason moved closer to her. He lowered his face to hers and looking directly into Alice's eyes he gritted his teeth and demanded, "You'll do as I say. Now give me the gun and make breakfast."

CHAPTER 43
I'D RATHER BE LUCKY THAN GOOD

Waiting to hear from the Las Vegas Police and the Nevada Gaming Control Board seemed to take an unusually long time. While Detectives Rich and Phelps continued to study the various reports, Julia was impatient and paced the floor. Desperate to move forward, but with little to do, Julia decided to make a quick run to the hospital and see Sam now that he was awake.

The cadre of police working the Mid-Morning Murder case assured Julia they'd let her know when they got a response from the Nevada authorities. "Don't worry, as soon as we hear anything, we'll call you," Roberta promised.

Approaching his room, Julia heard soft conversation but was unfamiliar with the voices. Two uniformed police officers stood by Sam's bedside, notebooks in hand, questioning him.

"Please give us a minute and wait outside. We're almost done," one of the officers said.

Julia stepped back into the hallway relieved to see Sam was able to speak and appeared to be alert. She whispered a silent prayer of gratitude. The police soon exited Sam's room and waved her in.

"Thank God you're okay. I've been so worried. Bring me up to date and tell me what the doctors say," Julia said almost tearfully.

"Hi! Well according to my medical team, I'm a very lucky man, so you can calm down. Looks like I'll be alive and kicking for a while longer." Sam's voice was weak and shaky, and he coughed while speaking. Julia reached for the plastic water container on his bedside tray and held it for him as he took a long drink through a straw.

"Thanks. They said the surgery went well; they removed the slug that was only millimeters from my heart." Julia could see talking was difficult for Sam and she didn't want to exhaust him.

"Take your time and you don't have to say anything more. I'm just glad you're awake and too stubborn to give in." Offering him another sip of water, Julia could see a smile cross Sam's face as he sank deeper into his pillow and closed his eyes.

"Rest now, and I'll tell you what we know," she said. "The bullet removed from your chest is a match to those used in the murders. Jason dropped his gun in the confusion and left it in your cottage. Phelps and Rich went to his apartment, grabbed his hairbrush, hoping to get a usable sample to see if there is a match to the DNA found in blood droplets in your cottage."

Julia paused giving Sam time to process this news. "They believe Maisie saved your life by attacking and biting the shooter as he took aim. Lunging at the shooter and holding on to his wrist, she diverted the bullet just enough so it would not be a direct hit to the center of your heart! Maisie's one of the heroes here. But then your poker buddies, the doctor, and the pharmacist got to your house in the nick of time to stabilize you and call the ambulance. So, you are a lucky man."

Sam nodded his head, indicating he heard and understood her account. "Yes, I told the two cops that just left that it was Montgomery. I recognized him as soon as he came into my house."

"There's more," Julia continued. "I think he's on the run and headed to his sister's in Las Vegas. We're coordinating with the Nevada authorities."

Sam painfully lifted himself onto an elbow trying to gain an upright position. "Don't do anything foolish, Julia. Leave it to the professionals. You mustn't get involved chasing after him. He's a dangerous man."

Sam's warning was interrupted by the ringing of Julia's cell phone. Holding the phone to her ear, she bit her lip and listened to Roberta Phelps. Julia silently mouthed Roberta's information to Sam who was desperately trying to hear the conversation.

"They have the sister's address. Got it through the Gaming Board. Sending officers to question her," was Julia's brief report to Sam.

"Sam, I gotta run. I'm going with them."

CHAPTER 44
THE ROAD TO VEGAS

"Did you ask the Las Vegas Police to meet us?" Julia breathlessly asked as she got into the back seat of Roberta's car. As soon as she heard that Alice's address was obtained from the Gaming Control Board and the information about the case was exchanged between the LAPD and Las Vegas authorities, Julia had rushed from Sam's bedside to join the detectives.

"No," Roberta explained. "We doubt Jason will be at his sister's place. We're not even sure that's where he was headed. We expect to question Alice, find out if he was there or if she knows where he might be. No need to call out reinforcements from the locals, at least not at this point. It's sufficient that we notified them of our activity, and they've agreed to assist if requested."

Julia accepted Roberta's reasoning, but strongly suspected Jason would be staying at his sister's place. "But what if he's there? Will you arrest him? Suppose he's not on the run because he believes we can't connect him to Alice?"

"Then he's a fool," Steven Rich interjected from the front seat. "He's smart enough to know we'd figure that out. If he got money from his sister or caught a brief nap there, he'll be long gone by the time we get there."

"He's no fool," Julia added. "If he's there, he is probably trying to cement an alibi or is planning on leaving as soon as he gets supplies, money, or a weapon. Or if he thinks we're on the way to arrest him he might even hold his sister as a hostage. Maybe we should ask for backup?"

Steven turned to address Julia and his tone was all business. "You need to relax and stay out of it. You're coming with us as a courtesy. You're not here in any official capacity. Stay in the car when we get there and let us handle it."

Feeling rebuffed and slighted, Julia settled into the back seat and remained silent for the rest of the trip. Finally, arriving at their destination, they parked the car near Alice's front door, approached her residence, and rang the bell.

"Yes, who is it?" Alice questioned.

Grabbing Alice's gun and her purse, Jason rapidly ducked into her bedroom at the rear of her residence. He hastily hissed at his sister, "Remember, don't say anything. You haven't seen me."

The two detectives, standing at the door, identified themselves and requested that Alice admit them. Opening the door Alice nervously gestured them in. Unsure how to respond or what to expect, Alice stood motionless waiting for the detectives to begin.

Roberta took the lead. "We have a few questions about your brother, Jason Montgomery. We'd like to talk to him. We hope you can provide some information. Do you know where he is? Has he contacted you?"

Alice almost paralyzed with anxiety, said nothing. Shifting her weight from foot to foot, she focused her eyes on her closed bedroom door. Phelps and Rich immediately understood Alice's silent message.

A noise from behind the bedroom door exploded with great force. Rapidly dragging a chest of drawers across the floor, Jason placed it against the door. He frantically wedged it under the doorknob hoping to slow the cop's entrance. Jason then leaped from the ground floor window to the back driveway. With Alice's gun in his hand, he feverishly searched Alice's purse for her car keys. Locating the keys, Jason jumped into his sister's parked car and drove away as quickly as possible.

The noise of the commotion, coupled with the detective's shouts to stop, alerted Julia, still sitting in the back seat of Roberta's car. Recognizing this was an emergency, Julia saw Jason wildly driving down the street. Without a minute to spare, she instinctively crawled over the seat, landing behind the wheel of Roberta's car. Reflexively she turned the car key and the motor roared into action.

Without any conscious thought, she threw the gear into drive and took off after Jason's speeding vehicle.

CHAPTER 45
RED ROCK CANYON

Jason already knew exactly where he was going to go to lay low – Red Rock Canyon. Located just 15 miles west of Las Vegas, it would be the perfect place to hide and only take a short time to get there.

The majestic beauty of Red Rock Canyon National Conservation Area defies description and covers more than 200,000 acres of nature's wonder, with enormous sandstone peaks, and huge red rock formations, reaching up to 3,000 feet to the sky. The grandeur of the park attracts visitors, hikers, and mountain climbers year-round.

Wild burros, bighorn sheep, and other animals roam the wilderness. In various areas of the park, plants and trees abound and although located in the high desert, there is cooling shade and freshwater.

Jason remembered that the park has hundreds of side roads and trails leading to campsites, countless smaller canyons, and year-round freshwater springs. He could bury himself deep into the area where he would be difficult to find. Physically fit and an experienced hiker and camper, Jason realized he could survive well there. Even without preparation or supplies, he was familiar with the location of water springs, the campgrounds, and the edible wildlife.

One can enter the park via Charleston Boulevard which turns into state road 159 and follow Summerlin Parkway for six and a half miles. The small entrance gate, staffed by Park Rangers, admits visitors after a small fee is paid. Maps of the park are provided and a leisurely drive down the thirteen-mile scenic loop road is suggested.

In remote areas, Native American petroglyphs decorate soaring rocky towers. Adventurers can explore this vast park and lose themselves to the imposing stillness.

As he sped down Summerlin Parkway, passing the gated communities, gambling casinos, and liquor shops, Jason devised a plan to stay hidden in the park for a week or so and then quietly drift away to some as yet undecided destination.

Now, some distance from Alice's house, he slowed his car. Convinced his rapid escape from her rear driveway left the detectives at a disadvantage, he began to relax a bit. Reasoning that his swift departure had provided a decent head start, he assumed the cops had lost precious time when caught by surprise, they first had to exit through Alice's front door and run to their car, parked in front of her apartment building.

"Good, I lost them," he whispered.

He was unaware the detectives no longer had their car, and that Julia had taken it. Nevertheless, Jason believed he made a clean getaway. Satisfied that he had taken off before they could follow, or even guess his destination, Jason was convinced he'd outsmarted the authorities once again.

"Dumb ass cops. They have no idea where I'm headed," he mumbled under his breath. Still speaking aloud, he cursed his sister, sure she let them know he was hiding in the bedroom. "I'll fix her ass when the right time comes."

Mentally reviewing his discussion with Alice, Jason was confident his sister couldn't give the detectives any information about where he was headed. Since it was a spur of the moment decision to seek cover at Red Rock, Jason's inflated belief in his infallibility grew.

"Okay, I'm in the clear. No need to attract attention by speeding. I'll just slow down and enter the park like any other tourist."

At this point, Julia was not far behind and as the pace slowed, she found her cell phone and auto-dialed Detective Phelps. "I got him, I got him," she shouted as Roberta came on the line. "Get a car and get your ass down here now. I'll hold him till you get here. We're entering Red Rock Canyon."

CHAPTER 46
ESCAPE AND PURSUIT

Shaken by the sudden development of this embarrassing situation, Detectives Phelps and Rich quickly analyzed their options. They realized they were in the midst of a giant blunder. They were without a vehicle. Roberta's car, commandeered by Julia, an unauthorized civilian, was now in pursuit of a dangerous felon, and they, the detectives in charge of the case, needed to quickly call for back-up and request transportation. Desperately trying not to appear foolish, the two LA cops sent out a request for assistance to the Las Vegas Police.

Previously notified that the LA detectives would be questioning a suspect's sister in their jurisdiction, and in the loop concerning the Mid-Morning Murders investigation, the LVPD was ready for any emergency. Fortunately, they were able to dispatch squad cars immediately to both Red Rock Canyon and Alice's address. It was understood they would pick up Detectives Phelps and Rich and head for Red Rock Canyon to join the team, already dispatched to search for the fugitive at that location.

Relieved reinforcements were on the way, Roberta stayed in constant phone communication with Julia, hoping to pinpoint Jason's exact location. She reassured Julia that help would soon arrive and again cautioned her not to do anything foolhardy or dangerous. Although Roberta was furious that Julia had taken off on her own, (in Roberta's car, to boot) she concealed her anger and would deal with Julia's impulsivity at a later date.

Nevertheless, Roberta did admire her gumption! Sure, Julia was a pain in the butt, but she was also worth her weight in gold, providing meaningful clues and insight. Roberta respected Julia's perseverance and her commitment to righting the wrongs of the world. In short, she liked her, and she would forgive Julia's headstrong misadventures.

Steven Rich also acknowledged and appreciated Julia's and Sam's participation and contribution to the investigation. But right now, he was gripped by fear for her safety. He, more than his partner, Roberta, worried that Julia's drive to apprehend Montgomery would endanger her. His concern centered on a recent conversation he'd had with Julia only a day earlier, almost immediately after Sam was shot.

"How do you handle the stress of the job?" Julia had asked him.

"Well, there's no doubt being a cop is stressful," he answered. "But I know I've had good training and I know I've got a good partner. Roberta's always there and she has my back. In the end, experience is the best teacher, and you have to trust all those elements working together will keep you alive. I've seen it all and feel pretty comfortable I can handle most situations."

"But you must face danger often? That's got to be scary," Julia remarked.

"There's always an element of danger present," he said. "But more often detective work is fitting the pieces of a puzzle together and figuring out what happened and who's to blame. You practice defensive measures, but the biggest part of the job is mental."

Julia shook her head nodding agreement.

"What about you?" he asked. "This has to be stressful for you too. I mean you see this Montgomery guy and work out with him on a regular basis. Do you sleep nights?" he asked.

Julia's answer was what worried Detective Steven Rich now, as he sat waiting for the LVPD backup team. Her words reverberated in his mind.

"My husband, Matt, insists that I practice target shooting regularly and carry a gun at all times now. When Sam was shot, Matt was so worried about my safety that he put the gun I forgot we owned, into my purse, and I've been carrying it with me ever since. I swear, if necessary, I'll use it."

CHAPTER 47
HIDE AND SEEK

It was early afternoon when Jason passed through the entrance gate to the park. Too busy planning his next moves, he paid no attention to the beauty surrounding him. Julia, still unobserved, followed a few cars behind.

Hoping to appear as just another tourist, Jason slowly drove down the scenic loop road. The mid-day sun, high in the sky, brightened the already vivid colors of the rocks and vegetation. Hikers lined the roadway, and several headed off in different directions seeking more challenging terrain.

Jason parked Alice's car in one of the designated lots and determined he would set out to climb one of the steeper and more remote paths. He briefly glanced at the park map the ranger had given him at the entrance gate. Believing there was no need to rush, he now took more time to study what might be the least traversed area. Sure he could manage a rough route, he decided to follow the two and a half-mile hike to Ice Box Canyon.

Described as "strenuous", the map guide indicated the trek would take the hiker to a cool and shady area where the canyon narrows and leads to a picturesque waterfall. Before reaching the cooler air and source of water, those who traverse this path must first cross open desert and then scramble over loose rocks and boulders. Jason figured there was little chance he would encounter other hikers there.

He searched the car's glove box and trunk to see if there was anything he could use while camped out in a remote area. He found a first aid kit containing the expected over the counter medical supplies and a few energy bars. He also found a flashlight, binoculars, a woolen blanket, and an umbrella. Upon further investigation, he found a large plastic tote bag, no doubt used for shopping by his sister, and thrust all these objects inside.

A smile crossed his face as he slid his hand into his pocket and touched the gun he had demanded from his sister only hours earlier. "Well, I guess that does it. Off we go," he mused.

Unobserved, Julia watched all this from a distance. She had none of the items Jason had located in his sister's car, but she reassured herself that she had the only thing necessary: she had a gun.

Julia reasoned her only advantage was surprise. She was confident Jason didn't know she was following him. But she understood Jason was stronger and was a more experienced hiker and rock climber. She knew she'd have to keep her distance, remain unseen, and still be able to communicate with the police by phone. She said a silent prayer hoping as they progressed deeper into the mountains, there would be cell phone service.

For the next two hours, both hikers marched separately, some distance apart. From her different hiding spots in the brush and bushes, Julia had seen Jason locate a stream. Once he moved on, she quickly dipped her hands into the same stream and drank hurriedly, hugging the ground, staying low to avoid detection.

In one area, the rippling water descended into a small cascade that created enough ambient noise to mask her brief phone call to Roberta. Amazingly, her cell phone indicated that she still had service in this remote area. She closed her eyes, hit the speed dial, grateful to learn Roberta and the other officers were in the park. As best she could, Julia, referring to her park map, told the police her location and gave them the name of the trail she was on.

Jason seemed unstoppable. He marched on showing little sign of fatigue. Julia was exhausted. As the heat of the day increased her stamina diminished, and she wondered how much longer she could continue. By sheer determination, she willed herself to go on, now fighting both fatigue and fear.

Finally, Jason stopped. Looking around, he spotted a large fallen tree and sat down to rest. Reaching into the tote bag he pulled out one of the energy bars and leisurely unwrapped it. He slowly took a bite, chewed effortlessly, and seemed to savor the dry flavorless nutrition.

From her secure and distant hiding spot, Julia thought this sight incredulous! She was staving and knew she'd eat the whole thing in one bite if she had it. Jason's nonchalance and unconcerned appearance shocked and frightened her. Doubt and apprehension gripped her, and she was enveloped in a cloak of uncertainty.

Images of Matt, Bobby, and Hilary flashed through her mind. Tears welled in her eyes, and she wondered how long they might grieve if she didn't return home. Consumed by emotion her body shook like tree leaves on a windy day. The pain of subjecting her family to such a loss ached and cut to her core, but she would not turn back.

Swallowing hard she tried to rid herself of these feelings of inadequacy and fright. "What was I thinking?" she asked herself. Her internal dialogue moved from one extreme to the other. First, she justified her swift decision to follow Jason as courageous and bold. But she quickly followed this self-talk with condemnation and self-accusations of stupidity and thoughtlessness. Amid these vacillating emotions, Julia sat on a large boulder trying to catch her breath as her internal argument continued.

"Damn him, he looks rested and happy, the bastard," she thought. "Roberta and her team better get here fast", she thought "or I'm a goner." Realizing she might not be able to keep up the pace, or worse yet, her presence might be discovered, Julia reviewed her options. "If Jason sees me...

A noise in the foliage immediately behind her startled her. She sensed sudden movement in the brush and jumped from her perch on the boulder and dove flat onto the ground, seeking cover. Trembling with fear she squinted her eyes searching for Jason. He was no longer seated on the fallen tree.

CHAPTER 48
YOU CAN RUN

Roberta, Steven, and three Las Vegas police officers labored under the strain of the difficult climb. They sensed they were closing in on their target and made sure to be as silent as possible. As they shortened the distance between themselves and Julia, they dared not use the phone to call her for more information. Even if the phones were put on vibrate, their voices could carry. Further communication was now a moot point.

The rapid response from the local authorities reassured both Roberta and Steven they were teamed with other professionals who seemed to know what they were doing and who were also somewhat familiar with the challenging terrain. The officers from both jurisdictions worked together well, without conflict or competition. They shared the same goal, the apprehension of Jason Montgomery. All of them, certain he was the serial killer they sought, were committed to bringing this case to a satisfactory ending.

The best the two LA cops hoped for was the swift location of Montgomery and an easy, uneventful arrest. Praying for her safety, they progressed up the trail and worried about Julia's ability to remain hidden. Certain they had reduced the gap between them and their target, they proceeded with extreme caution.

Only a few hundred feet away, and at the edge of a steep cliff, Julia crouched low and turned toward the noise that had frightened her. Fearful Montgomery had spotted her, she hardly took a breath as she turned to see what had disturbed the underbrush so close to her.

Her body ached and her breath was still as she shifted her balance and looked directly into the eyes of a huge Bighorn sheep. The animal had suddenly materialized behind her and seemed as stunned to see her as she was by his unexpected appearance. Locked eye to eye for only a few seconds, the ram turned and ran off kicking up loose rocks and debris, creating a swirl of dust. The sound of falling rocks echoed around the canyon below the cliff where Julia crouched. She immediately realized Jason, an experienced outdoor enthusiast, could hear the disruption and would focus his attention on the area from where the sound emanated.

Fear gripped her now, tightening its hold around her, clutching her in a powerful embrace. Desperately her eyes searched the area seeking any sign of Jason's location. She could feel, smell, and almost taste the extreme danger she faced.

She moved slowly, keeping low to the ground, and tried to conceal herself as best she could. She inched away from the cliff's edge and hid behind some bushes sprouting from a fissure in the rocky outcropping where she was perched. With tears in her eyes and desperation in her heart, she reached in her pocket and grasped her loaded gun.

CHAPTER 49
BUT YOU CAN'T HIDE

Jason's years of experience as a well-seasoned outdoorsman enabled him to recognize the abrupt noise coming from the other side of the cliff was a danger signal. Aware it might only be a large animal kicking up dust, he also knew it was possibly another hiker or the police he eluded at his sister's apartment. In any case, he'd take no chances.

Jason drew his gun. Reaching into the tote bag he hurriedly located the binoculars and suspended them around his neck. From a distance he carefully searched the area, looking for any sign of movement. Silently he inched up higher on the rocky terrain to improve his line of vision. As he ascended higher on the jagged cliff, he adjusted the binocular's focus and studied the topography. Careful to maintain his balance on the rocky incline, he dug in his feet to secure his position. The loose gravel and unstable stones tested his equilibrium. His footing was precarious but as he felt more secure, he continued his search.

Mentally he divided the area into several different quadrants and searched each methodically. Slowly and repeatedly, he scanned each quadrant. Sadly, no foliage, no tree limbs, nor any rock formations could conceal Julia's brightly colored blouse. Instantly Jason's focus was drawn to this unnatural burst of color. He lifted the binoculars, raising and readjusting the view-finder. First a pair of shoulders, then the neck, and finally Julia's face came into view.

"Holy shit! What the fuck is she doing here?" he whispered. Confused, Jason took a minute to consider the possible explanations. Under no circumstances was anyone to know his whereabouts and he would not tolerate anybody invading his privacy. He was a "Person of Intellect" and needed to protect his invincibility.

He was starting a new life. He was moving on and he was putting the past behind him. There could be no loose ends, no complications, no going back. He didn't stop to question why one of his clients was following him. The point was, he just didn't care. Cautiously, he lifted his gun and took aim.

Jason was momentarily blinded by the glare of the bright afternoon sunlight, which made him squint. "Shit," he cursed. "The one time I need my sunglasses I don't have them with me. Desperately he tried to adjust his focus trying to compensate for the interfering sun-light."

Drifting clouds and the few leaves swaying in the mild breeze created moving shadows and Jason found it difficult to zero in on his target. He squeezed the trigger, his bullet tearing past Julia only millimeters from her head. Terror gripped her, tightening her throat, but reinforcing her resolve. With nerves of steel, she drew her gun and returned the fire. Her aim was unpracticed and imprecise, but she refused to run. The gun's recoil surprised her, but she recovered quickly and was ready to fire again if she had to.

Shaken by the unfamiliar whizzing sound of her discharged bullet, Julia was dazed and didn't immediately understand its significance. Puzzled by the zinging noise the projectile made she crept up closer to better see Jason's location.

Julia's bullet ricocheted, glancing off a large, jagged rock formation producing the unexpected but typical ricochet whistling noise. Rather than penetrating the collection of boulders, the bullet bounced onto the formation. Striking the rock face at a critical angle, the bullet was now shredded by the impact. Shrapnel, together with shattered rocks kicked up a swirl of flying debris and dust. Damaged bullet fragments and pointed sharp-edged rough rocks exploded midair.

The deceleration of the bullet's velocity and energy did little to reduce the danger of the bullet's fragments and collateral damage. Although the velocity of the bullet was now slower than the expected collision velocity, the impact of the ricochet was overwhelming.

Flying rocks, bullet fragments, and dust particles hit Jason in the face and neck with unexpected force throwing him backward. He teetered momentarily on the edge of the cliff he had climbed earlier. As if in slow motion, he slowly rocked back and forth, battling to regain his balance. Within seconds, Jason Montgomery lost the battle and fell over the edge to his death.

CHAPTER 50
TIME TO UNWIND

Julia loved the beautiful tranquil setting of the newly finished koi pond located in a shady leafy area of the backyard. Building a koi pond had been a long-standing dream of hers and she was delighted by the work done by the gardener and the landscape design people.

Together with Matt and the children, Julia found satisfaction, enjoyment, and a sense of well-being as they fed the fish and watched them glide through the pond. The mesmerizing sounds of the pond's gentle waterfall and the drifting movement of the swimming fish created an oasis of restfulness and wonder.

The deep green of the garden foliage, the azure-colored water, and the gleaming flashes of the gold speckled fish, cast a spell of calm and peacefulness. It was here where Julia could put the past to rest and replenish her enthusiasm and resilience.

Although still bothered by occasional flashbacks and brief periods of intrusive memories, Julia possessed a remarkable ability to stay focused and remain positive. The ordeal of the last several months and witnessing Jason Montgomery's death did produce a mild case of post-traumatic stress disorder, but Julia responded well to treatment and quickly shed the most often experienced symptoms of PTSD.

Working with her behaviorist proved to be very beneficial. It was during these therapy sessions that Julia was encouraged to start new hobbies, join a support group, meet new people, and educate herself and others about how to overcome PTSD. Julia embraced these suggestions with enthusiasm and one of the many positive outcomes was the construction of the koi pond that lifted her spirits.

Slowly life was returning to the comfortable and familiar pattern of work, leisure, family, and fun. As the months moved from season to season, Julia's confidence and self-esteem grew. Her association with Roberta Phelps and Steven Rich developed into relationships of deep respect and professional collegiality.

Sam Malloy's complete recovery from the attempt on his life was a source of overwhelming joy for all. Sam's relationship with Julia and her entire family deepened so much so that the children loved him as if he were an honorary grandfather or much-loved uncle.

Finally, the Mid-Morning Murder case was officially closed. The paperwork, files, weapons, notes, and any other loose ends were all wrapped up and sealed away. It was finally time to unwind and have a little fun.

Julia readied things for the celebration. The weather was perfect for the happy event. Sunlight bathed the backyard garden, and a gentle breeze caressed the flower beds. Picnic tables, covered with brightly colored cloths, surrounded the pond. Comfortable lawn chairs, large patio umbrellas, and festive balloons framed the picturesque setting.

Humming a cheerful melody, Julia readied the tables for her guests. Platters, bowls, and pitchers, all filled with wonderful treats were carefully placed on the tables. Matt, Bobby, and

Hillary assisted in setting up decorations and games.

This joyous occasion did more than celebrate the end of the Mid-Morning Murder case. It gave special recognition and paid homage to the effectiveness of teamwork, perseverance, and commitment.

In the midst of this beautiful afternoon, Julia, Matt, Bobby, and Hilary were joined by Roberta, her husband, Marc, Steven Rich, Sam Malloy, and others who had worked on solving the case. Surrounded by the love, they embraced their friendship. One by one they each lifted their glass and toasted the success of their joint effort and the camaraderie born from that experience. Embracing each other, they shared true friendship.

As the sun began to set, the small group continued to celebrate. There was laughter, tall tales of past events, toasts to the future, and they all vowed to work together again. Matt and Julia and their guests were sure new adventures, new mysteries, and new challenges would greet them in the years ahead.

Whatever difficulties future tasks, trials, or obstacles might present, they would meet them together, undaunted, and unafraid.

ABOUT THE AUTHOR

Bara Rosenheck has had an active career working as a professional consultant and volunteer. Considered a "Change Agent" Bara has worked with small businesses, large corporations, and educational institutions to assist them in reducing bias, discrimination, and sexual harassment.

Bara Rosenheck Consultants was established in 2000 to provide expertise in reducing discrimination.

Rosenheck is an award-winning author. Her well-received novel, "Justice for Julia", is an Award-Winning Finalist in the Fiction Category of the 2019 Best Book Awards sponsored by American Book Fest.

Ms. Rosenheck and her husband, Dr. Arnold Rosenheck, live in Southern California.

OTHER BOOKS BY BARA S. ROSENHECK

COURAGE: IT'S MORE THAN LUCK

JUSTICE FOR JULIA

FOOLISH MOMENTS AND OTHER STORIES

Made in the USA
Middletown, DE
28 March 2023

27136005R00159